Where I'd
Like To Be

By the same author

Dovey Coe

Where I'd Like To Be

FRANCES O'ROARK DOWELL

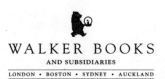

WALKER BOOKS
AND SUBSIDIARIES

LONDON · BOSTON · SYDNEY · AUCKLAND

First published in Great Britain 2004 by Walker Books Ltd
87 Vauxhall Walk, London SE11 5HJ

369592

2 4 6 8 10 9 7 5 3 1

This book has been typeset in Horley

Printed in Great Britain by J.H. Haynes & Co. Ltd

British Library Cataloguing in Publication Data:
a catalogue record for this book
is available from the British Library

ISBN 0-7445-8359-4

www.walkerbooks.co.uk

For Tori Ayeisha Ali Wedgeworth

Acknowledgments
The author would like to thank the following people:
Caitlyn Dlouhy, Susan Burke, Virginia Holman,
Kate Daniels, and Clifton and Jack Dowell

Chapter 1

When I was just a baby, a ghost saved my life. This is according to my Granny Lane, who I lived with at the time in a trailer on Roan Mountain.

Hurry, now, hurry, that baby is smothering, the shivery voice whispered into Granny Lane's ear. She popped open her eyes to find an old man dressed in overalls and smelling of black licorice gum standing next to her bed.

Granny Lane was up and running so fast she didn't have time to be scared. She raced to my crib in the corner of the living room, and sure enough, I was all tangled in a knot of blankets and couldn't breathe. After Granny Lane got me loose, she crept back to the bedroom, holding me tight to her chest, and flipped on the overhead light.

There was nobody there.

Granny Lane's landlady, Mrs. Treadway, said Granny Lane wasn't the first person in that trailer to be haunted.

"Folks used to see that ghost every few months or so, it seemed like," Mrs. Treadway told Granny Lane the next time she went to pay her rent. "They say it's John Edgerton, who used to farm this land. His wife and children burned up in a fire one day when he was gone off the mountain.

"It's been some time since old John Edgerton showed up in these parts," Mrs. Treadway went on, taking Granny Lane's check, folding it twice, and slipping it into her sweater pocket. "He must think highly of that baby of yours."

I like telling this story to people. It makes them think I just might be somebody special, even if I don't look it.

I told it to Murphy fifteen minutes after I first laid eyes on her. I wanted to give her my best story right up front because when a new kid comes into the Home, you've got to stake your claim quick if you want dibs on being friends. And I thought Murphy was somebody I might want to be friends with.

"Murphy's not my real name," were the first words out of her mouth after our housemother, Corinne, introduced her in the dorm. She leaned back against the hallway wall, her arms folded across her chest, not looking at any of us. "I don't tell anyone my real name."

"What's that junk all about?" Donita asked, already halfway out the door to dinner. "This girl don't tell no one her real name. You think anyone cares what your real name is, Murphy Oil Soap?"

Now that business about Murphy changing her name flat out interested me. I changed my middle name every few months or so to suit my mood. When I first met Murphy, my middle name was Jasmine. I thought Madeline Jasmine Byers had a nice ring to it. Before Jasmine, I'd tried out Amber, California, and, once, when I was six, Lollipop. My mama didn't bother to give me a real middle name of my own, which is why I was always on the look-out for a good one.

Murphy was the only one listening when I told my ghost story at dinner. Everybody else at the eleven-year-old girls' table had heard it already, more than once, and besides they were all too busy to pay any attention. Donita was cutting her dried-up chicken into tiny pieces so maybe it would look like she'd eaten some, and Kandy was lecturing Brittany on how many calories were in that lumpy mound of mashed potatoes on her plate. I had Murphy all to myself, which is just how I wanted it.

"So why don't you live with your grandmother anymore?" she asked when I'd finished telling my story, poking her fork at the pile of overboiled broccoli on her plate. "I mean, is there some specific reason she doesn't want you to live with her?"

I took a sip of milk. I was used to getting a more wondrous reaction to my story than the one I was getting from Murphy. "Well, Granny Lane got the diabetes when I was eight and her eyes started going bad, so I went to live with my aunt, and then she couldn't keep me anymore, and by that time Granny Lane had broke her hip and couldn't take me back, so I got fostered out. It's not like Granny Lane didn't want me living with her or anything."

"Oh," said Murphy. She sounded like she didn't care all that much. "Well, when I was a baby, my parents took me to Africa. My father carried me around in a sling everywhere they went, and people gave me presents. Once a boy no bigger than a weed handed me a dead grasshopper, and I ate it. It tasted like tuna fish, that tin can sort of taste."

"How do you remember all of that if you were just a baby?" I asked. "Most people don't have memories back that far."

Murphy shrugged. "I'm the sort of person who remembers everything. I don't know why." She speared a limp broccoli stalk with her fork and held it up. "What did they have against this poor thing anyway?"

"The cooks here hate all food," I told her, taking a bite of a stale roll. "It's not like they discriminate against the broccoli."

Murphy looked at me over her fork, like she was thinking about smiling and then decided against it. She pushed her plate away and asked, "So how long have you been here?"

"Five months," I answered. I was happy she was interested. "Since April. I came in about a month after Donita and Kandy. Brittany's been here since she was eight. I don't believe anyone's coming to claim her, and she'll never get adopted."

Those were the two things we were all biding our

time for at the East Tennessee Children's Home, either getting sent back to our folks or getting a new family altogether. I knew I wasn't going back home, and there wasn't much chance anyone was going to adopt an eleven-year-old girl as plain-Jane as me. I was just waiting out the years until I could pack my bags and move into a house of my own.

Leaning closer to me and cutting her eyes over at Brittany, Murphy whispered, "She smells terrible."

"Corinne is working with her on that," I whispered back. "I don't think Brittany gets the idea of personal hygiene."

Murphy shivered and frowned. You could tell by looking at her that personal hygiene was high on her list. Her curly brown hair was tucked neatly behind her ears, and she had a real clean smell about her, like apples and baby powder. Her clothes were nice. Maybe not directly out of a magazine, but better than your average foster-care child wardrobe. I know from personal experience that you're lucky to get clothes that fit when you're a foster-care child. Being fashionable is almost always out of the question.

Back in the bedroom all of us eleven-year-old

girls shared, Murphy began unpacking her cardboard boxes. She had four of them, which may not seem like much to you, but believe me, a lot of kids show up here with a paper bag full of nothing. I sat on my bed, which was right next to hers, and watched as she poked through first one box and then another.

"Don't you have anything better to do?" she asked, her head deep inside a box. "Play in traffic? Start a forest fire?"

"Nope," I said. I was just dying to see Murphy's stuff. I love stuff. One day I'd like to live in a big old house crammed floor to ceiling with stuff. "I'm fine right here."

"That's too bad," Murphy said, pulling out a lumpy pillowcase. She took a smaller cloth bag from the pillowcase, tucked it in her pocket, and heaved two of the unpacked boxes onto her bed. In a flash, she was up and teetering on top of them.

"Throw me that pillowcase, will you?" she asked, holding out her arms to get her balance. "I mean, as long as you're going to stare, you might as well be helpful."

"Aren't you afraid you're going to fall?" I asked.

"Those boxes look a little unsteady."

"I never fall. I don't believe in falling."

"What does believing have to do with it?"

Murphy shook her head, like she'd never met anyone so dumb. "Believing has everything to do with everything."

She grabbed the pillowcase from me and stuffed it under her arm. Then she pulled the little cloth bag from her pocket and carefully spilled its contents into her hand. "Thumbtacks," she told me. "In case you were wondering."

"I *was* wondering," I said.

"Why don't you go watch TV with everybody else?" Murphy asked, two thumbtacks clamped between her teeth, her words coming out cramped.

"I hate TV."

Murphy stretched up as far as she could and poked a thumbtack into the ceiling. "Me, too," she said. "TV's for idiots."

She pushed some more thumbtacks into the ceiling over her bed and began pulling things from the pillowcase: orange and black silk butterflies dangling from shimmery threads, a web of glow-in-the-dark stars, a silvery moon. One by one, she hung each item from a thumbtack, until she'd made a shining galaxy above her bed.

I was starting to feel more ordinary than usual, standing there watching Murphy. The only thing above my bed was a fluorescent light. I pondered the contents of my desk, wishing I had something breathtaking to pull out of my top drawer, like a singing canary or a pair of ruby red slippers, just something to make an impression. There were my drawing supplies, but I couldn't imagine anyone making a big whoop-d-doo about a bunch of pencils. My scrapbooks were interesting, at least to me, but I didn't like to show those around. I sighed, wishing I hadn't already told my ghost story.

"Do you need help with that?" I asked. She was straining to poke a loop of wire over a tack. The other end of the wire hung about a foot down and was coiled around a polished, blue stone. It was like she was trying to hang the smallest planet in the universe.

"Even if I did, I'd be out of luck," she said, grunting a little. "This is an incredibly special and rare artifact, and no one can touch it but me."

I stood on my tiptoes, trying to get a better look.

"Did you steal it from the Smithsonian?" I asked. "Or just borrow it?"

Murphy ignored my joke. She hooked the wire on the thumbtack and jumped down from the boxes onto the floor. Closing the lids to the boxes, she slid all but one under her bed. Then she took a seat at her desk, the same plain old brown particle-board desk that we all had, reached into the remaining box, and pulled out a paperweight, the snowy kind. "That stone was a gift from my parents, who were famous researchers. They collected artifacts from all over the world."

I sat down on my bed, feeling even less interesting than I had before. I didn't have a single artifact to my name. "Where are they now?" I asked.

Murphy plunked the paperweight on her desk. "Dead. They were killed in a car accident. I don't like to talk about it."

I looked at my feet. I didn't know what to say about dead people. "So is that why you're here?"

Murphy stood and slowly walked over to the sink. Her face looked yellow in the mirror, but then everyone's did. It was a terrible mirror to look into if you were trying to feel good about yourself. When she turned away from her reflection, her hands were planted on her hips. "I'm not supposed to be here," she said, her eyes narrowed. "I'm supposed to be living with my aunt. But she's somewhere in Europe and no one can get in touch with her."

Murphy looked up at the ceiling and blew out a few short breaths through her lips, so that the wisps of hair on her forehead fluttered out. It was the sort of thing a person might do to keep from crying. "I can't believe I ended up here, stuck in with a bunch of orphans."

"I don't think very many people here are orphans," I said. "Most people at least have one parent somewhere."

"Well, I don't." Murphy crossed her arms and stared up at the ceiling.

If Murphy were the sort of person who cried, she would have burst into tears at that very minute. But I learned that first night, Murphy wasn't the crying type.

Turns out, she was more the type to tell a bold-faced lie. Only I didn't know it then. I believed everything she told me.

Well, almost everything.

Chapter 2

Granny Lane always said, "God don't like ugly." She said it whenever I smart-mouthed her, and she said it when I made Roger Arnette a valentine out of black construction paper back in kindergarten. In fact, "God don't like ugly" was the main thing Granny Lane said to me when I did anything the least bit mean or rude.

But she also said, "Some people just feel like home," and she was talking about me. She was talking about Mr. Virgil Willis, too, who often as not was sitting across the kitchen table drinking coffee when she said it. Mr. Virgil Willis was Granny's best friend. "Just as good as a woman," she liked to say, "'ceptin' that he don't know how to sew or put up preserves to save his own life."

I can't tell you how many mornings of my life started out with me sitting at the kitchen table with Granny Lane and Mr. Willis, all of us eating oatmeal cereal and discussing the weather, just like a regular family. Mr. Willis always showed up first thing in the morning, and he always had some excuse for being there. "Thought you'uns might care to know there's a big storm headed up over the mountain," he'd say, taking off his cap and combing his fingers through his thick, white hair. "I know it 'cause my left big toe is like to fall off my foot, it hurts so bad."

"Mr. Willis, don't you know you don't have to have a reason to come visit," I told him one day, around the time I was six. "You're here so much, it'd be strange if you didn't show up."

Granny Lane shushed me and sent me to the bedroom, hissing "God don't like ugly, Miss Maddie."

Mr. Willis and Granny Lane were the first family I ever had, though I guess I should tell you up front that Granny Lane's not my real granny. She was just the old lady who lived next door when my mama decided to take a break from baby-raising, right about the time I was three months old. My mama never bothered telling Granny Lane who my daddy was, and she never bothered coming back to Roan Mountain, either. The last time anyone heard from her was when she sent the papers giving up her rights over me. After that, she kept quiet as quiet gets.

I've had a few families since Mr. Willis and Granny Lane, and they've been better in some ways, worse in others. One or two held on to me for as long as they could, and one or two couldn't wait to see me go. All I can say is, whenever I walk through a new door, I'm always looking for someone who feels like home.

I never thought that person might be Murphy.

"Corinne told me to give you the tour of the Home," I reported to Murphy on her second day there. "You need to learn your way around."

Murphy had been lying on her bed, staring up at that little, blue stone of hers. "I suppose so," she said. "Not that I plan on being here forever."

The next second she was out of bed and marching down the hallway, looking left and right, up and down, her hands behind her back, like she was visiting a museum.

"This is a fascinating tour so far," she said. "Very interesting."

"I don't think you need a tour of the dorm," I told her, ignoring her sarcasm and sliding in front of her. "You've seen the kitchen and the common room; you know the laundry room is downstairs. Let's go out and I'll show you which dorms are which."

I led the way down the brick path from our dorm to the road that circled around the different buildings that made up the Home. A plane engine roared overhead. I turned to Murphy and said, "Hey, maybe that's your aunt flying over to the airfield. Maybe she's come back to get you."

Murphy shook her head. "I predict that at this very moment my aunt is in Paris having tea at some very nice castle. Believe me, her interest in me is limited."

"So why would she promise to be your guardian?"

"Who knows?" Murphy said. "Maybe she was just being polite." She didn't sound all that mad about it, not like she had the night before.

We walked up the hill toward the Children's Dorm. Our dorm was the Older Girls' Dorm, and it looked a little bit like a house you might see in a regular neighborhood, red brick with cheerful windows. The Children's Dorm looked like an old motel: two stories, wide windows running across the front, air conditioners sticking out from every other one.

"All the little kids stay there," I explained to Murphy. "The boys are on the bottom floor and the girls are on the top floor. That low, brick building next to it is the administration building," I said, pointing. "You already know that's where the dining hall is."

I scooped up a rock and threw it at the dining hall door. "The thing that bugs me about those two buildings being next to each other is they don't match. It's like you've got the Sky High Motor Lodge next to Jones Ferry Elementary School. All I can figure is one got built way earlier than the other. It makes me itchy to look at them side by side."

"Things should fit together," Murphy agreed, picking up her own rock to throw. "Especially if you have to live with them every day. When we lived in this tiny village in South America, all the houses were exactly alike, small and pink, except for this huge, four-story town hall right in the middle of the village square. I walked a mile out of my way every day just so I didn't have to look at it."

I gave her a sideways glance. Murphy was the first person who'd ever understood how I felt about buildings. Of course, she was the only person I'd ever mentioned my ideas to, other than Ricky Ray, who was six and lived in the Children's Dorm. Ricky Ray hadn't given a whole lot of thought to the subject of architecture, though he always listened politely when I aired my views.

We trudged further up the hill past the Older Boys' Dorm, with its very own driveway and basketball hoop. Then we tramped down the road as it looped around behind the Older Boys' Dorm and back down the hill, passing the back of our dorm. In the middle of the loop was a playground next to a large garden area and some benches.

"We grew a lot of stuff there this summer," I said, pointing toward some drooping sunflowers. "It's a good place to come if you need to sit and think."

"I never think in public," Murphy said. "It makes people stare."

"Just about anything you do around here makes people stare," I told her. "There's not much privacy. You've got the staff and the houseparents, plus there's always somebody from the Department of Social Services running around. Don't expect to get away with too much."

"I'll put on my invisible shield," Murphy said, putting her hands up in front of her face, palms out. "Then no one will know what I'm doing."

"Just don't forget where you set it down after you take it off," I warned her.

Murphy nodded. "That's how I lost my last one."

We looked at each other.

I smiled.

Murphy did her best to keep from smiling.

"So is that it?" she asked, turning toward the Older Girls' Dorm. "Because there are things I need to take care of if we're through."

"That's it, I guess," I said. But neither of us moved. Our attention had been caught by two kids over by the swing set. They were seven-year-olds: a round, redheaded boy named Toby and a scrawny kid with glasses named Kevin. Toby was circling the swings, chanting, "Your mama ain't no good; she's got a butt that's made from wood," over and over. Kevin's hands were stuck tight to the chains of his swing, like Toby's words were holding him prisoner there.

Toby wasn't saying something that kids everywhere don't say, on the bus, on the playground at school, even out behind the Sunday School trailer over at the First Baptist Church. But when you're a foster-care child, someone saying something about your mama can hurt as bad as stepping on a nail. Mothers are a real sensitive topic. Once you get older, you learn how to hide your hurt better. But a little kid like Kevin didn't stand a chance.

Without saying a word to each other, Murphy and I marched in step over to the swing set. Murphy planted herself in front of Toby. "Hey!" she yelled at him. "Leave that kid alone! You're a bully, and I don't like bullies. So scram! Get out of here! Run like the wind!"

You could see Toby take a quick measure of the situation. He looked at Murphy, who was a good foot taller than him, if not but a pound or two heavier, and then he looked at me. I folded my arms across my chest and glared.

Toby took off like a shot.

Poor old scrawny Kevin tried to say something, but he only managed to stammer, "I . . . I . . ."

Murphy rolled her eyes. "What are you talking to me for? Go eat some graham crackers, why don't you?"

Then she turned to me. "Now is that it?"

"Yep," I said. I trailed her over to the Older Girls' Dorm and up the back door stairs. Inside, Murphy turned and looked at me.

"Are you following me?" she asked.

"I live here, too," I said, shrugging. "So I guess I am."

"Well, don't."

Murphy made a beeline to the bathroom, leaving me standing open-mouthed in the hallway. Back in our room, I stood in front of the mirror, looking at my yellow reflection, my arms folded across my chest. First I glared, just like I did at that kid Toby. Then I grinned. Out on the playground, me and Murphy had been a team. She could deny it all she wanted, I didn't care.

I knew what I knew.

Chapter 3

After dinner that night, I took my championship rodeo belt buckle off my belt and started polishing it, the way I do every evening. It's oval-shaped and silver, with a picture of a horse rearing up on its back legs, and I put it on first thing every day, along with jeans, a T-shirt, and a pair of Keds tennis shoes. I'm not by any stretch of the imagination a fancy dresser, but I think my rodeo belt buckle shows a little flair. It was a gift to me from Mr. Willis, who found it at a flea market over in Cranberry one afternoon.

"Where'd you get that?" Murphy asked when she saw me hold the buckle up to the light and inspect it for marks. "Did you ever ride in a rodeo?" She got up from her bed, where she'd been staring up at the ceiling like she was studying it for a test, and walked over to my desk. "Can I see it?"

I handed her the buckle, suddenly a little scared she was going to steal it from me and claim it as her own. A girl in second grade had taken my favorite drawing pad from me once and went so far as to tell everyone she'd drawn the pictures in it. I'd considered almost everyone I met a little untrustworthy ever since.

"A friend gave it to me," I told her. She peered at it closely, as though she were making sure it wasn't a fake. "I know it's on the small side, but I'm pretty sure it's real."

"Oh, it's real all right," Murphy said, nodding like an expert. "I knew a boy once who was a famous rodeo star, and he had twenty or thirty of these in a trunk in his room. I'd know if this one were fake."

She walked back to her bed still carrying the belt buckle, and I had to keep myself from jumping over to snatch it back from her. When she went on talking, it was like she was having a conversation with the buckle, not me, since she never once looked me in the eye.

"This boy grew up on a ranch in Arizona, so

riding horses was like walking to him, and breaking colts was something he'd been doing since he was a little kid. He started riding in rodeos when he was really young, too, and he was pretty good, but he wasn't the best, and he was the kind of kid who wanted to be the best at whatever he did."

"So what did he do?" I asked, inching my chair closer to her bed, in part to let Murphy know I was interested in what she had to say, in part to lunge for her if she tried to make a break for it with my belt buckle.

Murphy balanced the buckle on the palm of her hand. "He went east to live with his aunt. I don't know if you ever heard of Ocracoke Island, but that's where he went because that's where they have wild ponies. Worse than wild. Those ponies were feral."

"Doesn't *feral* just mean *wild*?"

Murphy shook her head, still not looking at me. "You might think so, but they're two different words completely. *Feral* is wild to the furthest degree. No one could ever break those ponies or even get near them. But this boy, he figured out how to talk to the ponies. For hundreds of years, people had been trying to break the feral ponies of Ocracoke Island, and this boy finally learned the secret. After that, he was never bucked from a horse again. If you know anything about rodeo, you'd know his name."

I had to admit that I didn't know a thing in the world about rodeo. "But what *was* the secret?" I asked, reaching for my buckle and feeling relieved when Murphy handed it back to me.

"Poetry," Murphy said. "He told them poems, and after awhile they got so hungry to hear them, they'd do anything he asked."

Murphy's story made me want to draw something, which is usually how a good story affects me. I was about to ask her if she wanted some paper and pencils, thinking she might want to draw, too, but before I had a chance, she'd already flipped off her desk light and headed out of the room.

Later, when I was lying in bed, I tried to figure out whether Murphy liked me or not. Every time I thought she wanted to be friends, she up and walked out the door. Maybe she thought I was too boring to be her friend. After all, she'd traveled all over the world and had artifacts hanging over her bed. What did I have? A belt buckle? No wonder she wasn't the least bit interested.

Just when I'd halfway decided to give up on ever being friends with Murphy, her voice reached across the dark alley between our beds.

"Hey, Maddie," she whispered. "Look at the clock."

The digital clock on my desk read 11:11.

"What about it?"

"Make a wish. Whatever you wish for at 11:11 will come true."

I thought about it for two seconds. "Okay, I wish for a million dollars."

"Don't tell your wish! Keep it to yourself. And make it serious."

"A million dollars isn't serious?"

"Of course not," Murphy said. "It's not even important."

Now the clock read 11:12.

"You'll get another chance in the morning," Murphy whispered. "So make it something good."

I closed my eyes and thought of good things to wish for. I would wish for Murphy to like me, even if she was exotic and interesting and I was just myself. I'd wish for Granny Lane to get her eyesight back and for Mr. Willis to win the *Upper Room* magazine essay contest, which he tried for every year. And right before I fell asleep, I decided to wish for a million dollars. Maybe it wasn't important, but it sure would come in handy.

The next morning Corinne and her husband, Dan, loaded up the dorm van with everyone who went to the middle school and drove us to school. We usually had to ride the bus that pulled up at the end of the drive every morning at 7:30, but Corinne and Dan had to take Murphy to the front office to sign her in, so we all got to ride. I made sure to sit next to Murphy so I could point out the few spots of interest between the East Tennessee Children's Home and Lawton Crockett Middle School.

"So do you know whose homeroom you'll be in?" I asked her as the van neared the school.

"The paper they gave me says I'm in room 124," Murphy said, leaning her head against the window. She sounded bored with school already. "Mrs. Cattrell. But I switch out for math, to the accelerated class."

I was impressed. Not many of the foster-care children I knew were in the accelerated classes. I was in accelerated reading, but that's just because I'd been reading since I was four. Mr. Virgil Willis taught me. Every morning he'd bring over the *Johnson City Press,* and we'd read through the sports section. As a result, I have an encyclopedic knowledge of baseball, which hasn't come in handy so far, but you never know.

"I'm in Mr. Sanders' class. We sit next to Mrs. Cattrell's at lunch," I told Murphy, "and they don't care if we mix up tables. So we can eat together."

"Girl, you talk too much in the morning," Donita said, reaching out her foot to kick me lightly on the shin. "Fact is, you talk too much all the time."

I knew she was just joking, because if she hadn't been, she would have kicked me a lot harder. Me and Donita had always gotten along real well, even if we weren't best friends. She and Kandy had naturally gotten matched up together, on account of them arriving at the Home at the same time and both of them from Knoxville. But I liked how Donita always had some interesting project going on. Last summer she started a green bean business, growing beans in our garden and selling them to the congregation of the First Baptist Church after Sunday services, and lately she'd been talking about taking a correspondence course in how to speak Japanese so she could be an international businesswoman one day.

"I'm just trying to give Murphy some important information about her new environment," I told Donita. "I'm trying to be helpful here."

"Miss Murphy Oil Soap can eat lunch without your help," Donita said, kicking my other shin. "She don't need you there to hold her hand."

"I'll see you at lunch, don't forget," I called to Murphy after we arrived at school, and she was headed toward the main office with Dan and Corinne. She nodded without turning her head, but I was pretty sure she'd heard me.

When lunchtime came around, I carried my tray, with its taco, salad, beans, and Jell-O square, out into the cafeteria, searching for Murphy. I expected that she'd be sitting all by herself, looking lonely, hoping that I'd be there any minute to save her from the humiliation of eating alone.

Which was why it was such a surprise to see Murphy with her head thrown back, laughing like she'd heard the funniest thing in the world, and Logan Parrish beside her chewing on a taco, smiling and smiling.

Chapter 4

One day last spring, when the beautiful May morning was begging all us kids to come out and play, and our teacher Mrs. Harris kept hinting she was going to turn us loose for recess ten minutes early since most of us had done real well on the math test, Logan Parrish threw a fit because he'd gotten a 98 instead of a 100. He stood in front of Mrs. Harris's desk waving his hands around like a crazy person, while everyone in the classroom moaned and groaned and yelled out, "C'mon, Logan!" and "Save it for after school, Logan!"

By the time Logan was done, we could look out the window and see all the other fifth grade classes already on the playground. We'd missed seven minutes of a beautiful spring day recess on account of Logan Parrish, but he ignored the boos that came his way as he walked back to his seat, the 98 unchanged on the top of his test paper, still fussing and fuming under his breath.

That was just the sort of misfit Logan Parrish was. He didn't even try to get on anyone's good side, the way poor old pimply Molly Dietz did, handing out Twinkies at lunchtime and writing book reports for people. You couldn't even feel sorry for him. He couldn't care less whether you did or not.

"What are you laughing about?" I asked, setting down my tray, trying to hide my disappointment that Murphy was eating lunch with the most despised person in the sixth grade. "Did I miss a good joke?"

Murphy tucked a stray curl behind her ear. "Oh, we were just discussing Mrs. Cattrell. She explained how to multiply square roots in class today. It was pretty painful."

"She has to use a calculator, if you can believe it," Logan said, shaking his head, which as usual was covered up by a grungy blue Fraley's Feeds baseball cap. "It's so pathetic."

I examined my taco. Math was not my strong

point. "So how's your first day going, anyway?" I asked Murphy. "I mean, besides the square roots and all?"

"Okay," Murphy said, taking a bite of pinto beans. "I've seen worse schools than this one, I guess."

"You should join the band," Logan told her. "There are a few people who aren't morons in band, unlike the rest of the clubs in this school."

He had a stringy little piece of lettuce hanging from his glasses, but before I could think of a polite way to mention it, Murphy reached over and flicked it off. "There seem to be some low-flying vegetables in the air today," she said, smiling at him, her green eyes shining. Logan went red, and he looked at Murphy all googly-eyed, like she was a present Santa Claus had just dropped on the table in front of him.

Murphy leaned over and tapped her fork on my tray. "Hey, Maddie, can we have boys over at the dorm? I mean, can Logan come over?"

"Ricky Ray comes to visit me in the afternoon sometimes," I said. "So I guess so."

Logan wiggled his eyebrows at me. "Is Ricky Ray your boyfriend?"

"Ricky Ray is six," I told him. "He's a little young for romance."

Looking at his watch, Logan said, "My mom's picking me up for a dentist's appointment in five minutes. Should I tell her to drop me off at the Home this afternoon, around four?"

"Sure," Murphy told him. "It's the first dorm as soon as you come up the driveway. I'll be waiting out front."

"Waiting to do what?" I asked as we watched Logan walk out of the cafeteria, his two-ton back-pack hanging off his right shoulder, his trumpet case in his left hand. "What on earth could you think up to do with Logan Parrish?"

"Well, there's math homework, for one thing," Murphy said, popping her Jell-O with a spoon. "And looking for something to do, for another. I'm the sort of person who always needs something interesting to do, wherever I am. I was raised that way."

"But why Logan Parrish?" I asked. "What makes you think he'll be interesting?"

Murphy began packing up her stuff. "What you don't understand about Logan is that he's a frog prince."

"A what?"

"A frog prince. A person who once was a frog but who got the right kiss and turned into a prince. Can't you tell he used to be an amphibian? He's still not used to being human, that's perfectly clear to me," Murphy said, shoving a notebook into her backpack. "It's like he's not of this world, not of that world."

I'll tell you, my head was starting to spin. For one thing, who in the world would kiss Logan Parrish?

I stood and picked up my tray to take it over to the trash. "I think you're confusing Logan Parrish with some fairy tale," I told Murphy. "Trust me, they're two entirely different things."

"Don't you believe that magical things can happen?" Murphy looked at me like she was dead serious and expected a serious answer in return.

I was stumped. "I guess I never thought about it," I said. "But I haven't seen much evidence to prove it."

"Oh, there's more to everything than the eye can see," Murphy informed me. "I thought everybody knew that."

Chapter 5

I was in a bad mood when Ricky Ray came over that afternoon, which he sensed right away. Little kids are smarter than anyone ever gives them credit for.

"Let's look at the books, Maddie," he said, tugging on my sleeve. "It'll make you feel happier."

We were sitting in the common room, on the brown couch that had coffee stains all over it. It had been donated by someone from the First Baptist Church of Elizabethton, which is the church that sponsors the Children's Home. Whoever donated this couch needed to cut down on the caffeine, that much was clear.

"I don't feel like it, Ricky Ray," I said. "You have to be in the right mood for the books to work."

I was in a horrible mood. How could I be friends with Murphy if she was going to be friends with Logan Parrish? The very thought made me feel irritable up one side and down the other. She was sitting on the front steps that very minute, waiting for him so they could make some stupid plans that would probably cause Logan to wiggle his eyebrows some more. I hated to even think about it.

Ricky Ray leaned his head against my arm. "Maddie, Maddie, oh, won't you go get the books?" he pleaded in a sing-songy voice. "It makes me so very, very, very happy to look at the books."

I couldn't deny Ricky Ray anything. "Okay," I said. "But not all afternoon. I've got things to do. Important things."

Ricky Ray just smiled. Nothing made him happier than to look at my scrapbooks of cut-out pictures, and since he was the only person I ever showed them to, it was like we had a little club together. I knew I could trust Ricky Ray to treat the books with the proper respect. Even though he was only six, he was careful with things. One of the first times I'd ever noticed him, he was trying to repair an ant hill he'd stepped on by accident. He would never mess up anything if he could help it.

I guess you could say I'd sort of adopted Ricky Ray. Or maybe he'd adopted me. After I'd been at the Home a couple weeks, I started walking around the big circle every afternoon, looking at all the build-ings and wondering how long it would take me to save up to buy my own house. I pretended each step I took earned me ten dollars. One afternoon, I heard a little voice behind me say, "Thirty-three, thirty-four, thirty-five . . ."

I turned around and saw a blond-haired kid with bangs flopping in his eyes, his expression as serious as a preacher's. "What are you doing?" I asked, not mad, just curious.

"Helping you count," he said. "Sometimes you count out loud when you're walking; that's how I know that's what you're doing. What are you counting, anyway?"

"Footsteps, dollar bills, a down payment on a brick house with a white fence around the front yard."

"You don't have to buy a house. You can come live with me and my mama when she comes to get me. She won't mind a bit."

Ricky Ray started walking again. "Thirty-six," he said. "Thirty-seven, thirty-eight . . ."

We got up to four hundred and forty-two that day. At the end of it, Ricky Ray said, "We could get bunk beds, when you come to live with me and my mama. You can even have the top one."

There was something about him—the way he flicked his bangs out of his face with a shake of his head and looked at me with his straight-ahead smile, like he just knew one day we'd be living the high life at his mama's house—that made me want to pull him into a big bear hug then and there. Instead I said, "You can have the top bunk, that's okay."

His face lit up. "Cool!" He started running toward the Children's Dorm. "See you tomorrow!" he called. "Maybe we'll get up to five hundred!"

And that's how me and Ricky Ray ended up adopting each other.

"Here," I said, throwing two black-speckled scrapbooks onto Ricky Ray's lap, after I got them from my room. "I hope you're happy now."

The *Book of Houses* and the *Book of People* were the only two scrapbooks I kept anymore. I used to have a bunch more, including the *Book of Animals* and the *Book of Nature,* but when I moved to the East Tennessee Children's Home I became so busy with other activities that I didn't have time to keep up with all of my books. Looking for pictures to cut out can eat up your whole day if you're not careful.

Ricky Ray pulled the books close to his chest and wiggled in his seat. "Come on, let's do a story."

I couldn't help myself. I snuggled next to Ricky Ray on the couch and opened the *Book of Houses,* breathing in deep its wonderful, papery smell, just as good as a library book's in my opinion, maybe better. "See that one?" I said, pointing to a contemporary home in the Victorian style. "I found that in Saturday's real estate section. I love it so much. Just read the description: 'Master bath with Jacuzzi, cathedral ceilings, eat-in kitchen, and many more must-see amenities!'"

Ricky Ray pulled open the *Book of People* to his favorite page. "She's going to live in that house," he said, pointing to a very tanned model in a black bikini with a boa constrictor wrapped around her shoulders like a mink stole. "That is the best house for her. Her name is Crystal."

Ricky Ray always named the girls in the *Book of People* Crystal. Crystal happened to be his mama's name, if anyone cared to get psychological about it.

I leafed through the *Book of Houses,* seeing if there were any other new pictures Ricky Ray hadn't seen. He liked to be kept up to date. "Oh, look at this one," I said. "It's a 1930s-style bungalow with hardwood floors and ceiling fans. I found that on Sunday."

But Ricky Ray was too busy looking for his other favorite cut-out people to pay attention to my attractive bungalow in the "Great, Great Location!" "Here's the first one you ever cut out, back at Mrs. Estep's house," he said, pointing to a picture of a teenage girl in platform shoes that was on page 1 of the *Book of People.* "That was after Randy Nidiffer taught you how to do your own books."

Ricky Ray had memorized practically every story about my life that I'd ever told him. I figured that was Ricky Ray's way to make it sound like we'd always known each other and that all of my stories were his stories, too.

"Randy Nidiffer was like a brother to you,"

Ricky Ray continued as he leafed through the pages. "You sure wish he would write you a letter."

"I decided I don't care anymore about that," I lied, rubbing my finger across a ranch-style house to make it stick better to the paper. "It doesn't matter so much anymore."

"Oh, well, that's good," Ricky Ray said. "I sure miss him, though."

"You never even knew Randy Nidiffer, you silly thing," I said, leaning over and poking him in the belly.

"I know. But I miss him anyway."

I chewed on a cuticle, a habit Corinne was trying to break me of. Maybe it shouldn't have surprised me that Randy Nidiffer had stopped writing. Maybe you shouldn't expect boys to write you letters, even though it sure would have surprised me if Mr. Willis had quit clipping out the baseball statistics from Sunday's paper to send to me April through October. But I had to admit when Randy's letters stopped after only two, it felt like a piece of me had withered and died on the vine. Randy Nidiffer had always felt like home to me.

Randy Nidiffer had been the only other foster-child at Mrs. Theresa Estep's house when I lived there, right before I came to the Home. He had wavy, golden-brown hair that spilled over his forehead and freckles everywhere you could see. He made terrible grades and talked back to adults whenever he got the chance. He refused to dress for gym, he stole ice-cream sandwiches from the case when the cafeteria ladies had their backs turned, and he smoked cigarettes.

The secret of Randy Nidiffer was that he was a great artist. To the best of my knowledge, no grown-up had ever discovered this about him. After I'd lived at Mrs. Estep's house for a few weeks, Randy started showing me his sketchbooks. I remember being startled by his pictures of hands, which looked so real I once had a dream they came alive and started brushing my hair with a silver-plated hairbrush.

He also made notebooks using cut-out pictures from magazines and newspapers, and he had stories for every picture he'd ever cut out. "Now this boy here," he'd say, pointing to a picture of a boy clipped from a cereal ad, "his name's Thomas Lee Oakwood, and he's no good. He used to be good, but no matter how good he was, his brother was always better, at least on the surface of things"— and then he'd point to a picture of a boy who looked like he was dressed for Sunday school— "His brother's name is Cameron Lee Oakwood. Everybody loved Cameron so much, but they had no idea that sometimes he stole money off his daddy's dresser and that he'd pawned some of his mama's silver at the Bull's-Eye Pawn Shop down on Bristol Road."

When I first knew Randy, all his notebooks were of people. I was the one who gave him the idea for a book of houses. Mrs. Estep had dragged us to the Food Lion along with her two scrawny boys, but Randy and I chose to sit on a bench beside the gum ball machines instead of trailing her past the produce and the Deli Fresh Meat Counter. A rack of glossy real estate magazines stood next to our bench, and I picked one up to look at the pictures of the pretty houses. I'd always lived in houses that were run-down and crooked and wore an unhappy look about them. The houses in the real estate magazines were cheerful and new, and the scent of fresh lumber seemed to come right off the pages.

"These would be real pretty in a notebook," I told Randy. "These could be where the people in your other notebooks lived."

After that, Randy and I collected real estate magazines whenever we could, and we spent almost every afternoon cutting out pictures. We made the first *Book of Houses,* and I started on my own *Book of People* and several other books as well. Mrs. Estep thought we were crazy. "Don't leave your magazines near them kids," she'd tell anyone who would listen. "They'll cut 'em all to pieces."

Now Ricky Ray flipped through my latest *Book of People,* pointing out all the different Crystals that he found there. "This Crystal has blonde hair and this Crystal has black hair. . ." he went on in his little-boy drone. I pulled him over onto my lap and rested my chin on the top of his head. All the time I wished I was twenty-one so I could adopt Ricky Ray for real and live in a friendly, white house with green trim and a big backyard for playing ball in. That was the right sort of place for a little boy like Ricky Ray.

"I don't know why you won't believe me!"

Logan Parrish's voice came crashing into the hall-way. "There's nothing to do in this town or this county, and the people here are morons. You're going to have to run away to Johnson City if you're looking for something to do!"

"Well, let's go then," Murphy said, walking into the common room. When she spotted us on the couch, she said, "Don't tell me it's the famous Ricky Ray right here in my very own dorm!"

Ricky Ray looked confused. He was just a little boy and didn't understand people joking around, even when they were doing it in a nice way.

"I bet he's helping Maddie with her homework," Logan put in. He grabbed the *Book of People* out of Ricky Ray's hands. "What *is* this? Paper dolls?"

I held out my hand and gestured for Logan to give me the notebook, barely containing the urge to pull out every last piece of his hair. He must have sensed I was reaching my limit, because he handed it right over.

"But really," he said, sounding serious. "What is that, Maddie? An art project?"

I shrugged. "It's hard to explain."

Murphy sat down next to me and tapped a finger

on the *Book of Houses*. "May I look?" she said in the politest tone I'd yet heard her use. I shrugged again, and Murphy took the book from me.

She turned the pages slowly, which made me nervous. I was afraid she'd say something that would ruin the *Book of Houses* forever. People can do that, you know. They can take the things you love and twist them around with a few words so you can't bear to ever look at them again. That's why I hardly showed the books to anyone if I could help it. I had to protect the things that meant something to me. I put my arm around Ricky Ray and pulled him closer.

I was afraid for the both of us.

Murphy started shaking her head, still looking at the book. "This is so great," she said. "This is really, really neat."

She looked up at me. "Where did you get the idea for this? I love these houses! I can't wait until I live in a real house again."

I nodded. I understood what she meant. I couldn't wait to live in a real house, either. And one way or another, some day not too far away, I hoped, I would.

Chapter 6

A beam of light played against my eyelids, sending red streaks through a dream I was having about an old brown dog of Mr. Willis's named Gus. When I opened my eyes, I saw Murphy sitting up in her bed, grinning a big grin, a flashlight in her hand.

"Let's build a house," she said, aiming the light in my face again.

"Cut it out with the flashlight," I hissed. "I'm halfway blind from it already."

Murphy put the flashlight directly under her chin, turning her face into a ghoulish, glowing mask. "Don't you think building a house is a great idea? It may be the best idea anyone has ever come up with in this room, although that's probably not saying much."

"I don't know the first thing about building a house," I said, sitting up and pulling my knees to my chest. "I wouldn't even know where to start."

Murphy pointed the light at a pile of books next to my bed and ran it up and down the spines. "Let's see, I count nine, no, ten library books there, which means you know how to use a library card. We'll go to the library, check out some how-to books, and we'll have a house built in no time. A small house. I helped my parents build an adobe hut once in New Mexico, when they were studying the Hopi Indians, so I already know a lot about it. Believe me, Maddie, human beings have been building houses for thousands of years. Anyone can do it."

"I don't know, Murphy."

"Okay, maybe not everyone can do it," Murphy said, training her light on Brittany and then Kandy. "I'm not saying they could do it. But we could, you and me."

She turned the flashlight on me again. "Say you'll do it, Maddie."

There was something in her voice, almost like she was pleading.

How in the world could I say no?

The next morning we were on our way to the Elizabethton Public Library, with Ricky Ray, Logan Parrish, and Donita right along side us. It was a beautiful late September Saturday, the sky high and blue, the trees beginning to show their colors.

It would have been a perfect day, if not for the fact of Logan Parrish. Asking Logan along wasn't my idea, you can be sure about that.

"Hey, Logan, have you ever heard Maddie's ghost story?" Murphy asked, a few blocks away from the library. Donita, who'd heard the story on several occasions, groaned, but Ricky Ray grabbed my hand and said, "Tell it again, Maddie!"

So I did. I was happy Murphy wanted to hear it, especially since I wasn't sure she'd been as impressed as she should have been the first time I'd told it to her.

The minute I finished, Logan asked, "So why don't you still live with your grandmother? How come you're at the Home?"

"Granny Lane got diabetes and her eyes started going bad," I said, sounding like I was reciting from a script. "Everyone thought it best that I stay with people more able to meet my developmental needs."

Murphy put her hand on my shoulder. "Why are you even bothering to answer that question?" she asked. Then she turned to Logan. "It's absolutely none of your business why Maddie is here, or why any of us are. That's personal information."

Logan Parrish turned red as a sunset, which I found very satisfying. You could tell he didn't want to do anything to get on Murphy's bad side. He kept looking at her with a dopey grin every five seconds it seemed like, and it was starting to get on my nerves. I wished he'd go fall in love with somebody else.

"What did the ghost look like, Maddie?" Ricky Ray asked, same as he always did, tugging at my shirt. "Weren't you scared?"

"I was just a baby, so even if I had seen him, I wouldn't have remembered," I explained. "But I didn't see him."

"I'd be afraid that ghost was going to track me down," Donita said. "We ain't that far from Roan Mountain. He could find you, check to see how you were doing."

"He wouldn't hurt her, though," Murphy said, turning to face Donita. "Why would he hurt somebody whose life he saved?"

"A ghost is a ghost, friendly or not," Donita said. "Whichever way, I bet Maddie don't want to shake hands with one in the middle of the night."

Donita was going to the library to check out a book on dolphins for a science report. When Corinne heard that Murphy and I were going to the library, she told Donita to scoot along with us. It was fine with me, but Donita didn't look any too happy about it. From what I could tell, Donita hadn't warmed up to Murphy one bit over the past few days.

The Elizabethton Public Library used to be the Elizabethton Post Office, back in the old days when they made post offices in the beautiful style of high ceilings and gleaming floors. Once everything turned modern, though, they built a new post office over by the Wal-Mart. The new post office had gray linoleum and ceilings of regular height, and it was hard to get too excited about going over there to buy stamps if you should need some, which I rarely did.

On the other hand, I was always in need of books to read since I got through a stack or two of them a week, so I was happy that they turned the beautiful, old post office into a library.

The minute we walked in, I went straight to Mrs. Dugger, the head librarian, and asked her where the house-building books were. Mrs. Dugger didn't blink an eye, but marched us right over to the shelves featuring books on home repair and the like. I like a librarian who doesn't ask too many questions and respects your privacy.

Everyone but Donita, who'd gone to find dolphin books, grabbed handfuls of books with titles such as *Designing Your Own Home* and *Contemporary Home Plans* and lugged them over to one of the long, oak tables by the reference section.

"This one's got a lot of house plans in it," Logan said, flipping through the pages of one of his books, "but I don't see any directions for how to build the house itself."

"That's easy," Ricky Ray said. "You just get hammers and nails and wood. Everybody knows that."

"I think it's a little more complicated than that," Logan told him in a superior tone of voice. "Although you have the basic idea, I guess."

Murphy stood up. "I'll go see if they have any books with instructions. We'll probably need several different books if we're going to figure out how to build a house."

The books in my pile mostly showed plans for the sort of houses you saw out by the new mall in Johnson City. They were subdivision houses with big garages and windows that lay flat against the outside walls. Over the years I myself had developed a liking for houses with more character, although I understood why people might want to buy a house that was fresh and new and completely their own. I spent a lot of time wondering about the girls who lived in the dorm before me. It seemed strange to think how their stuff once cluttered up my desk and their clothes filled the closet I now shared with Murphy, Donita, Brittany, and Kandy. Sometimes I worried about those girls, what might have happened to them.

"My books give a lot of measurements," I told Logan and Ricky Ray after I'd gone through the whole stack. "But that's it."

Murphy came back to the table at the same time that Donita was settling in at the far end of the table with a pile of books I guessed were on the subject of dolphins.

"Here's a bunch of stuff on renovations and adding extra rooms," Murphy said, letting an armful of books tumble down on the table. "But nothing that says how to build a house, A to Z."

Donita looked up from her notebook. "Y'all really serious about building a house?" she asked. "I mean, you got some land around here?"

I hadn't thought about where we would build the house. We'd gotten so caught up in the idea of building a house at all, we hadn't really discussed the details. I looked at Logan. "How big is your yard, anyway?" I asked him. If he was going to be a part of this, he might as well come in handy.

Logan reddened again. "It's pretty big," he said, like it almost embarrassed him to admit it. "But, well, I don't think my parents would let us build another house on it."

"Why don't y'all just build a fort?" Donita asked, sounding practical. "'Cause I used to live with this family where the man was a contractor, and he had to hire lots of people to build his houses. No offense, but I'm not sure y'all could build a whole house by yourselves. Now a fort, that's a different story. I could even help you get the boards and the supplies for it."

Murphy sighed. You could tell she really wanted to build a house. But Donita was right, and we all knew it.

"So Logan," Murphy said after a moment, "we know that building a house on your property is out of the question, but how about a fort? A big fort?"

"Sure!" Logan said, sounding relieved that he could be of some use after all. "The back of our property is mostly woods. My parents would probably like it if I built a fort, as a matter of fact."

"Why's that?" Donita asked.

Logan shrugged. "It's the sort of thing a normal guy would do. My parents would like for me to be as normal as possible. Like right now, my dad's mad because I decided to be in band instead of trying out for football."

"You don't look unnormal to me," Ricky Ray said nicely.

"Abnormal," Murphy corrected him. She turned to me and mouthed the words *frog prince*.

Donita bounced her pencil on the table a couple

of times. "You hanging out in the woods all after-noon with this bunch is going to make your folks happy?"

"They'll be glad I have some new friends," Logan said. "My mom is always getting on my case about making more friends."

"How many friends do you got now?" Ricky Ray asked.

Logan looked down at the table. "I had one, but he moved last summer."

"Well, if your parents will let us build a fort in their yard, they must be nice folks, which means you're probably a nice person, too, underneath it all," Donita said, standing up. "I'm going to check out these books, and then we'll go see my Uncle Wendell. He'll help us out."

We all followed her to the checkout desk. Without so much as a how-do-you-do, Donita was part of the plan.

Chapter 7

"I didn't even know you had an uncle here," I said to Donita as we tromped up the sidewalk toward the center of town. We were passing the Limestone Grocery, which was hardly a grocery store at all, just one room of wooden bins filled with produce from Sonny Baldwin's farm. Today the outside bin featured mostly pumpkins and yellow squash.

"He's not really my uncle," Donita said. "But black folks in this town are few and far between, in case you haven't noticed. I think he just wants me to feel like I've got some of my own kind around if need be."

"Could we grow pumpkins at our fort?" Ricky Ray asked, catching up with us. He had hung back a few seconds at the Limestone Grocery and was clearly under its influence.

"I thought I told you, we'll be building the fort in the woods," Logan said, as he couldn't believe how dumb Ricky Ray was. "Pumpkins need sunlight to grow. Lots of it."

I grabbed Ricky Ray's hand and pulled him along with me. "Logan Parrish, I believe you have impressed us with the fact that you know more about many things than a six-year-old boy does," I told him. "You're a regular encyclopedia. So why don't you quit picking on Ricky Ray?"

"Holy cow!" Logan said, holding up his arms as if surrendering. "The kid asked a question."

"Which you could have answered in a polite and respectful manner," I pointed out.

Logan Parrish shrugged, but he looked more than a little humbled. I was hoping we could embarrass him all the way out of the building project. There had to be someplace other than Logan Parrish's backyard to build a fort.

Donita made a sharp left onto Watauga Avenue. "Turn here," she said, leading us past the Elizabethton Savings & Loan and across the railroad tracks. We passed Trivette Coal Company, the name of which would make you think it was a large business of some importance, but really it wasn't much more than a shack where Mr. Lindberg Trivette kept his office and a small supply of the coal that he sold by the truckload or the sack. Mr. Trivette was about ninety years old, and he spent most of his day sitting at his desk reading novels. I ran into him a lot at the library, when we were both checking out our weekly supply of books. "You read any of them Thomas Wolfe books I been telling you about?" he always asked, and I always had to shake my head no. I picked up *Look Homeward, Ange* once, but the first few paragraphs didn't really draw me in.

"Uncle Wendell, you there?" Donita called out. We were nearing Potter's Used Auto Parts and Misc. Supplies, which looked to me to be a former gas station. It had that design to it, with a roof that came off the main building to shade a rectangle of concrete covered with oil spots, making it appear like a map of some far-off planet. All that was missing were the gas pumps themselves, but you could see where they might once have been bolted to the concrete.

"Hey, Uncle Wendell," Donita called again. She turned around and said to the rest of us, "He's getting on in years. I don't think his hearing is all that good."

"Ain't nothing wrong with my hearing," a man said, walking out from what I guessed was the main office. He must have been Mr. Potter. "I'd wager good money I hear a sight better than you do, little gal. Now come give your old deaf uncle a hug."

Donita went over to the man, who was wearing a dapper hat from the 1950s, a brown cardigan sweater, and wing-tipped shoes, and squeezed on him. "How you doing, Uncle Wendell?"

"My day just got a whole lot brighter, that's for sure," Mr. Potter said, patting Donita on the head. "You bring some friends with you?"

"These are some people I live with, except for that tall one over there," she said, pointing to Logan Parrish. "His name's Logan Parrish, and he lives over on Snob Hill. I understand his daddy's a judge."

Mr. Potter nodded. "I voted for him in the last election, as a matter of fact."

Logan half smiled, half smirked. You couldn't tell if he was proud of his daddy or if he would have voted against him if he'd been of age.

"That's Maddie," Donita continued her introductions, pointing at me. "And that curly-headed girl is Murphy, only that ain't her real name, but don't ask me why that is; and the little boy is Ricky Ray."

"Goodness, you got quite a crowd with you today," Mr. Potter said. "Y'all just stopping by for a visit, or do you have some business with me?"

"We're going to build a fort at that one's house," Donita told him, pointing a finger again at Logan. "We're going to need some supplies, maybe some tools, too."

"I've got tools," Logan said. "I've got my own toolbox. And we can use my dad's stuff, too. He never does."

Mr. Potter nodded. "So you'll be needing some lumber, some nails, that sort of thing." He turned toward his office, motioning with his arm. "Well, follow me out to the back; we'll see what I got on hand at the moment."

We crowded in through the door to the office and

then squeezed out through the door to the garage. Snaking through the maze of tires and hubcaps and rusting car batteries, we followed Mr. Potter out a back door and found ourselves in a kind of backyard, a fenced-in square of hardpan dirt with clumps of onion grass struggling to grow around its edges. Here we were greeted by an oddball collection of open-mouthed ranges and refrigerators that had clearly seen their heyday many years before, not to mention washers and dryers and a chorus line of vacuum cleaners. At the far end of the yard, cinder blocks two and three deep kept different lengths of sawed lumber off of the ground.

"Who's the main architect here?" Mr. Potter asked us. "Any y'all know something about building a structure?"

Logan stepped forward. "I know a little bit," he said, sounding sure of himself.

"Good, good," Mr. Potter said. "Now, any of y'all any good at math?"

This time Murphy stepped forward. "I'm in the advanced math group at school," she told him. I waited for her to say something about building an adobe hut in New Mexico, but she didn't mention it.

"Good, that's what I like to hear," Mr. Potter replied, sounding even more enthusiastic. "You done any geometry yet?"

Murphy nodded. "A little. At my old school."

"Well, then, you two come over this way and let's discuss what you children will need." He turned to Donita. "Baby, you take the rest of them and fill five or six coffee cans with nails. Be sure to get a variety of sizes."

Ricky Ray nudged me. "Maddie, I ain't got no money. How're we going to pay?"

I shrugged, looking at Mr. Potter, who smiled. "Y'all don't have to pay for it. I like to help out my little niece when I can."

"We could barter for it," Murphy said. "Not Donita, since she's your niece, but the rest of us. I mean, we might need a lot of supplies. I don't want to take advantage."

Mr. Potter smiled again. You could tell he liked Murphy. "You might be on to something there, missy. I could use me a few hours of help around here. I appreciate that you want to be square on your debt. That's a good habit to have."

Logan Parrish opened his mouth, but before he

could say a word, I cut him off. "Don't even offer to pay for this, Logan. We've already worked out a real good deal."

"I wasn't going to offer to pay for it," he stammered. "I was just going to say that I could come by on Wednesday afternoons after school, if he needed help then."

I felt my face go red. "Oh," was all I managed to say in reply.

"Go get those nails, children," Mr. Potter said, saving me from further disgrace. "We'll work out a schedule later."

It took the good part of an hour for Mr. Potter, Murphy, and Logan to figure out what lengths of board we'd need for building. They also had a long discussion about techniques for making a fort stand up straight and last through a windy season.

After helping Donita fill two coffee cans with nails, I roamed around the appliances and dreamed of the kitchen I'd have in my own house one day. I wanted one of those kitchens that had a big wooden block in the middle, for your husband to chop up vegetables on while you were cooking dinner.

"So how are we going to get all this stuff to my

backyard?" Logan asked, after he and Murphy and Mr. Potter had picked out what appeared to be enough lumber to build at least three forts and set it aside in a special pile. It was, I hated to admit, a sensible question.

"We can haul it in my truck," Mr. Potter said. "You and your daddy can help me unload it, get it to wherever it needs to go."

Logan nodded. "Sure, that'd be great. My dad's probably not home, but I'm pretty strong. Do you want to do it now or wait until you're ready to close up?"

Mr. Potter smiled. "There is one main reason I went into business for myself, children," he said, ushering us back through the garage toward the front, "and that is because when you are your own boss, you can close up shop at a moment's notice."

We all helped to load up Mr. Potter's truck, and then Donita hopped into the front seat, while the rest of us rode in the back with the neatly bundled wood and the other supplies. I peered through the truck's narrow rear window at Donita and Mr. Potter, and a feeling came over me that was both sad and pretty. I couldn't exactly name what it was.

Chapter 8

I wanted to be building that fort every spare minute of the day, every day, but I had obligations, and I knew better than to sneak out of them. Corinne and them were always keeping an eye on me to make sure I was behaving myself. I'd been known to get into a little trouble now and again, nothing much, mostly just cutting up in class. But add that to the fact that I was an abandoned child who didn't even know who her daddy was, and it was enough to have people look at me cross-eyed every time I sneezed too loud.

Thursday afternoon I was at my Journey through the Mind meeting, wishing like crazy I was out at the fort. Journey through the Mind was a sort of zany-brainy organization where kids got together to put on skits and solve problems for competition. I always looked forward to JM practice, though I have to say the fact that Logan Parrish was in JM took some of the shine off it for me. He was the sort of person who always thought his ideas were best, even when everyone else was thinking in the opposite direction. It could tire you out after awhile, arguing with him.

I could tell from Logan's antsiness that he wished he were at the fort, too. He kept hopping from one foot to the other and couldn't get focused on the project at hand: the construction of a time machine that would send our team into three different periods in history, where we'd have three different problems to solve.

It was strange to have something in common with Logan Parrish. Every once in awhile our eyes would meet, and we'd almost smile at each other. For the first time in my life, I didn't feel the urge to snatch that Fraley's Feeds blue cap from his head and shove it in the closest washing machine.

We'd been working on the fort for almost a week. That first day Saturday, though, I thought we were done before we even got started. To begin with, we'd had to sit through a lecture on safety from Logan's father, Judge Martin Parrish, who'd stood in front of us in a pair of lime green pants, a jaunty golf cap on his head, smiling a big cheesy smile that he must've learned running for elected office. He'd told us how he and Mrs. Parrish had always supported the Home through their church, and that he was happy to be able to help us with this project of ours, but, basically, if we busted our thumbs with a hammer, not to come crying to him.

"I hope building this fort will teach all of you responsibility," he said, like he'd read a report somewhere that we were the biggest bunch of ne'er-do-wells in the county. "And I hope it will teach Logan some much-needed social skills."

Murphy gave the Judge her own cheesy grin. "We appreciate you letting us use your yard, sir," she said. I thought I saw her batting her eyelashes when she said it.

After Judge Parrish left, we stood there in the clearing in the woods behind Logan's house, our shoes all wet from dew on the grass, the pile of boards in front of us waiting to get hammered and nailed; and our faces were big zeroes, just blank as could be. There didn't seem to be any way to begin.

Then Donita took a few steps forward and turned around to face us. "All right, now, there ain't no need to panic. Let's start at the starting place. What do we need to get going with this?"

Ricky Ray squinched his eyes and twisted his cap in his hands, trying hard for the right answer. "Wood?"

Donita nodded toward the stack of lumber. "Okay, we got the wood. What's next?"

Taking in a deep breath, then letting it out slowly, Ricky Ray said, "Nails?"

"Nails," Donita agreed. "I see them cans of nails, but let's put 'em in a specific spot." She looked around quickly, then grabbed a long pine branch near her feet and walked it a couple of yards away from the pile of boards. Then she moved the cans of nails so they were lined up against the branch. "Okay, this is where we keep the nails. Nails don't get moved away from here. Everybody got that?"

We all nodded. "Okay then, Ricky Ray, what's that leave us with?" Donita put her hand on Ricky

Ray's shoulder, like she had all the faith in the world he was going to come up with the right answer.

"Tools!" he yelled at top volume, and you could tell he felt confident as could be, having gotten the first two things on the list right. "We got to have tools, don't we, Donita?"

"That's right, honey, and we got plenty," Donita said. She turned to Logan. "You got a tarp of some sort back in your garage? Garbage bags will do, if that's all you got. Can't have no tools lying on the wet ground."

Ten minutes later, we were organized. The air around us seemed lighter from pure relief, like we thought this fort might just get built after all. Before we went to work laying out the boards for the floor, we took a few minutes to study for the millionth time the plans Mr. Potter had helped Logan and Murphy draw up. Then, hammers in hand, we got down to the business of putting that fort together.

Do you know the smell of raw lumber? It's the freshest thing you can imagine. Every time I pounded a nail further into a board, it was like a little puff of perfume came out, and I breathed it in as hard as I could. "They ought to put this smell in a bottle," I said to no one in particular. "I'd pay top dollar for it."

"You know why trees smell the way they do?" Murphy asked, looking up from her hammering.

"Sap?" Logan guessed. "Chlorophyll?"

Murphy shook her head. "Stars. Trees breathe in starlight year after year, and it goes deep into their bones. So when you cut a tree open, you smell a hundred years' worth of light. Ancient starlight that took millions of years to reach earth. That's why trees smell so beautiful and old."

I thought it sounded like poetry, what Murphy had to say about the trees. I shook my head. I could talk a blue streak, but I could never say things the way Murphy did.

I saw Donita roll her eyes, but she smiled, too. She held a bunch of nails between her lips, so it was a strange sort of smile, but it seemed real enough. Murphy appeared to be growing on her, though that didn't mean they were living in harmony night and day.

Right around lunchtime, Murphy backed away

from the building site and peered toward it, her hand shading her eyes. "You know, I think we should have some turrets," she called out. "Like on a castle. I stayed in a castle once, with my parents, and it was really nice. Well, it got cold at night, but we just piled on the quilts and were warm as toast."

"You're kidding, right?" Donita asked, not even bothering to look up from where she was hammering in a joist hinge. "We'll be lucky if the walls stand up. We can't be adding no towers for Sleeping Beauty."

I looked around at what we had so far, just the skeleton of the floor and the boards for one wall lying on the grass, waiting to be nailed together. "I have to admit, it's hard to imagine adding anything fancy to what we've got," I said.

Murphy came a few steps closer. "Do you want this thing to look like a shoe box? Completely boring?"

Donita stood and crossed her arms. "I want it to stand up and stay standing," she said, sounding firm on the matter. "I don't think we need to be having ridiculous dreams about what could be."

Logan jumped into the middle of the fray. "All right, ladies, all right! Let's break it up. No cat-fighting on the premises, if you please."

Murphy and Donita glared at him. Then they looked at each other and cracked up. They laughed so hard they were choking on their laughter and pounding each other on the back. Logan stood to the side and looked confused, until Murphy finally caught her breath and looped an arm around his shoulder, grinning at him. "Logan the Peace-maker," she said.

Logan shuffled his feet. "I was only joking," he said, frowning. "Nobody ever gets my jokes."

I watched Murphy and Donita laughing together, and it made me feel shy. I wished me and Murphy could cut up that way sometimes. We did a lot of stuff together, not even counting the fort, but I still couldn't help but wonder if Murphy really wanted to be my friend or if she just needed someone to pass the time with until someone came to collect her from the Home.

Over the next few days our hammers kept pounding, and the air was a mix of sounds—bird-song fluttering between the ring of metal on metal and wood. Every once in awhile we'd hear the putt-puttering of Mr. Potter's old truck pulling up in the Parrish's driveway, and pretty soon he'd be walking around the edges of the fort, giving us building tips.

"Y'all know where your windows are going to be?" he'd asked us Monday afternoon. Murphy and I were marking the bottom boards of the frame so we would see where to place the studs, the boards we'd nail plywood to for the walls. "That's going to influence how many studs you need to mark for."

Donita was counting out nails. "We don't need windows, Uncle Wendell. A door ought to do us."

"We have to have windows," I protested. "Otherwise it'll be like hanging around in a dungeon."

"Listen to me on this one, Maddie," Donita insisted. "You got windows, you got rain coming in the windows. You got snow coming in the windows. You got God's creatures coming in the windows. Windows are more problems than we need to be dealing with here."

Mr. Potter put his hand on Donita's shoulder.

"I got some strong plastic covering you can put over the windows, baby. When the days get short, you'll be wanting some light in there while you can get it."

He turned to the rest of us. "All right, children, let's talk about how you make yourself a window."

Logan was the one who knew the language of houses: king studs and trimmers, rise, run, and span. He was the one who showed Ricky Ray how to drive a nail into a board, bending down low so he could guide Ricky Ray's hands. "My grandfather taught me that there's two ways to nail pieces of wood together," he explained the first day. "There's face nailing, which is when you pound the nail through one board directly into another board, like this." He gave an expert tap of the hammer, using just the right amount of force to shoot the nail through one piece of wood and into the next.

"But sometimes you've got to toenail," he said next, and that cracked Ricky Ray up. "I got ten toenails," he said to Logan. "I know all about toenails."

"Well, I wouldn't recommend doing to your toenails what I'm about to do to this nail, okay?"

Ricky Ray nodded, all serious, as Logan showed him how to drive a nail down at an angle to make a T out of two boards. "That's pretty hard to do," he said when he finished, "so you better let me help you if you need to do any toenailing."

I stood there watching with my mouth hanging open. It was like a new Logan Parrish had been born before my eyes. With a hammer in his hand, Logan didn't just seem like a normal person, he was downright heroic.

We were starting to get somewhere: we had a floor, the side walls and end walls were ready to go, and the corner posts were up. I had it all in my mind's eye as I sloshed a brush dipped in silver paint across our Journey through the Mind time machine, wondering what Murphy, Donita, and Ricky Ray were doing at that very minute. We'd accomplished a lot so far, but it would probably be another week before the fort was finished.

"Do you think we ought to paint the outside?" Logan Parrish had come to stand beside me, his hands jammed in his pockets, his feet dancing in his shoes.

Any innocent bystander would have thought Logan was out of his head. Obviously we were already painting the outside of the time machine. But I knew exactly what Logan Parrish was talking about.

"I just don't want to take forever for it to be finished," I told him, waving my brush and accidentally flecking his arm with silver paint.

Logan nodded, rubbing his arm on his jeans and making a big, silvery smear. "Me, either. But at the same time, I have a hundred ideas for what we could do to it to make it completely great."

"Like put shutters on the windows," I said.

"Or build steps up to the front door," Logan said, excitement threading its way into his voice. "And I was thinking that it couldn't be that hard to figure out how to put window-panes in the windows. And what do you think about trying to find a woodstove? It's going to get cold soon. We could cut a hole in the roof for the stovepipe."

"Logan?"

A woman wearing a bright blue sweater and gray slacks stood at the foot of the stage, looking up at us, her eyebrows raised as though she found what we were doing just the slightest bit amusing. "It's 4:45, honey. I promised Daddy dinner would be on the table by six. He's got a board meeting tonight."

"Is that your mom?" I whispered.

"Yeah," Logan whispered back, not sounding all that happy about the fact.

I looked at her a moment longer. "She doesn't really match you, does she?"

Logan shook his head.

Looking down at Logan's mother, I could see she didn't have a frog bone in her body. Mrs. Parrish was immaculate. Her frosted blonde hair was cut in a neat bob, not a strand out of place. Also, you could just tell she had a pocket organizer and a cell phone in her purse. Mrs. Parrish was the sort of woman Granny Lane had always admired. "Oh, that one, she's got her act together, now don't she?" she'd say. Granny Lane wasn't the least bit organized herself, but that didn't stop her from liking others who were.

The way Mrs. Parrish rattled her keys lightly, signaling that it wouldn't be a good idea to test her patience, let you know right off that her act was more together than most people's.

"Can we give Maddie a ride home?" Logan asked his mother. "She's one of the kids working on the fort."

Mrs. Parrish gave a brisk nod of her head. "Of course. But both of you, please. Dinner at six means dinner at six."

It felt funny to walk out of the building matching step for step with Logan Parrish. It suddenly occurred to me that we might even be friends. Logan gave me a half-grin and rolled his eyes at me as his mother held out her keys and beeped open the car door locks of a spruce green people carrier.

Logan's little sister, Marcy, was sitting in the front seat talking on a play cell phone, running her hand through her floppy, blonde curls as she spoke. When Mrs. Parrish introduced us, Marcy put her hand over the receiver and whispered, "Sorry, can't talk right now. Important call."

"Caroline?" she spoke into the phone. "Lunch on Tuesday?"

Mrs. Parrish smiled. "Marcy's in the second grade, and already she's quite the social butterfly."

I looked at Logan, who was struggling to get his seat belt on, his face going red from the effort.

I was pretty sure he had to be adopted.

"So Maddie, Judge Parrish says that all of the children building the fort come from the Children's Home," Mrs. Parrish said as she pulled out of the parking lot behind the auditorium. "How long have you been there?"

"Since April," I told her. "Before that, I was living with a foster family over in Blountville."

"It's a good thing you came over here," Mrs. Parrish said. "The schools are much better. And the Children's Home is excellent. Our church sponsors a scholarship. We sent one young man from the Home to Cornell University."

"I'm sure he was happy about that, Mrs. Parrish," I said. Outside the car, the trees seemed to rush past us in a blur of green and yellow, the leaves just beginning to change over. I imagined a boy on a college campus that smelled like autumn and wood smoke, and a little shiver ran through me.

"It was a wonderful opportunity for him," Mrs. Parrish agreed, glancing at me in the rear-view mirror. "So is it your wish to be adopted?"

Logan looked at his mother. "Mom, that's pretty personal."

"Not at all," Mrs. Parrish said, brushing Logan's remark away with a wave of her hand. "Maddie knows she's in the foster-care system. I'm sure she's given some thought to the question, and if she hasn't, then perhaps she should. I'm sure all foster-children consider adoption."

I nodded. "I've thought about it some. Mostly what I want is my own house. Besides, the people who want to adopt eleven-year-old girls are few and far between."

"That's a problem you hear about a great deal," Mrs. Parrish said. "Even for children as young as two years old."

I liked the way Mrs. Parrish spoke to me, like she considered me her equal. You could tell she wasn't the sort of person who wasted time talking to people not worth the effort.

"How about your parents, Maddie?" Mrs. Parrish had pulled the car up to the foot of the Home's driveway and now turned to look straight at me. "Are they completely out of the picture? Or is there a possibility of reconciliation?"

"I don't have parents," I told her. "But I still have my Granny Lane up on Roan Mountain. I've got family lots of places, come to think of it," I said, picturing Mr. Willis and Randy Nidiffer in my mind. "Granny Lane used to always say, 'Families are made, not born.' I guess that's how I feel about it, too."

I pondered Logan's family as I walked toward the dormitory. It was hard to see much of his mama in him, the way she was just about perfect and Logan was anything but.

If he wasn't adopted, maybe Logan got his frog genes from his daddy, I thought, pushing open the dormitory door and breathing in the warm scent of the dryer coming up from the basement. I pictured Judge Parrish hopping around a courtroom, his long black robe flying up to show those lime green pants underneath.

I laughed, wondering what old Murphy would think about that.

Chapter 9

It was beautiful.

Maybe if you were a world-famous architect or interior decorator you wouldn't think so, but if you were one of us, you couldn't take your eyes off of that fort.

Saturday morning, two weeks after we had set out to the library to begin our task, Murphy, Donita, Logan, Ricky Ray, and I stood in front of the end result of our many hours of labor, silent at first, and then we couldn't stop talking.

"It sure is a lot more like a house than I thought it would be," Donita said, pacing back-and-forth, nodding her approval. "I think the roof makes it seem like it could be a house. We should put shingles on it, though."

"And we have to paint it." Logan slapped a wall with the flat of his hand. "Maybe green, so it would be camouflaged. I don't want this place easy to spot."

I had so many plans for our fort, they were spilling out of me like water from a faucet. I sat down on the fort's front step and started going down my shopping list. "The next time Corinne and Dan take us over to Wal-Mart, I'm going to buy us a pitcher and a big jar of instant tea, and that way we can have something to drink whenever we want. I'll get some gallon jugs of water, too, to make the tea with. And maybe a rug. Do you think we could get wall-to-wall carpeting somewhere?"

In the middle of all this noise, Murphy gave a dramatic clearing of her throat. We all turned to look at her. "I think this is an important occasion that should be marked somehow," she said, and the rest of us nodded. "Maybe if we got together in a circle and somebody said a few words."

"Something exactly right," Ricky Ray put in.

"Something just right," Murphy agreed. She looked at me. "You read a lot of books, Maddie.

Maybe you know the right thing to say."

"Give me a few seconds," I told her, thinking she should be the one to say something; she always had such amazing things to say. But she'd handed me the task, so I walked away from the fort to stand behind a sycamore tree, searching for the words like I might find them on the ground among the leaves and the acorns. I peeked around the tree and took the long view of what we'd built. The fort was nestled in a stand of trees, the dappled shadows of leaves falling across its walls. What was once a clearing of dirt and moss and rocks was now home to this collection of boards and nails. I wished that it had an address people could write letters to.

I didn't have many words to say about it, which was unusual for me. When I walked back to the fort, I motioned for everyone to join me in a circle. I looked at the window and imagined a curtain of blue calico blowing through it.

"Today is a good day," I said. "And we have made a good place. May it stand for a long time among these trees."

I thought that keeping it short was best. I could tell by the look in everyone's eyes that they agreed with me. We smiled at each other, and then Murphy said, "It's time for the ceremonial march inside, beginning with the youngest."

And so Ricky Ray, beaming so hard with pride I thought he might just burst into beams of light, led us inside.

Standing in the center of the room, I looked up at the ceiling and turned slowly around. Who would have believed we could've done this almost entirely by ourselves?

None of it was easy work, and it took us two weeks of squeezing in time between school and practices and church activities, two weeks of hiking from the Children's Home up Allen Avenue, over Dewey Payne Road, and a quarter-mile through the woods that ran along the edge of Hampton's Dairy Farm, hiking until the woods thinned and we could see the backyards of the houses in Logan's neighborhood through the black walnut and sycamore trees, and then counting one, two, three, four houses, until we were in the farthest back part of Logan's backyard.

I would have made that hike five times a day. Six times a day. It was that worth it to me.

The inside of the fort was one room, ten feet

wide and fourteen feet long. This was plenty of space for everyone to stretch out and get comfortable, which everyone immediately did. You could look into any person's eyes and see that they coming up with dreams for the fort. Me, I wanted a place for cubbyholes, the kind that my kindergarten class had, where we could keep our things and maybe leave each other mail.

Even without furniture, the fort was the kind of place I liked to be. There were two windows, one east and one west, and a nice breeze blew through, bringing with it the smell of the woods. Wednesday, after we'd gotten the roof raised with the help of Mr. Potter, we'd all pitched in and painted the walls a soft off-white with paint Logan had borrowed from his parents' basement. Now the walls seemed to glow with light.

"I believe I'd like to live here forever," Ricky Ray sighed, leaning back against the wall and breathing in deep a mix of freshly painted walls and autumn trees.

The rest of us just nodded yes. We didn't even need to say it out loud.

After that first day, we were all at the fort as

often as we could be. Murphy and I got into the habit of hiking up there after we worked at Mr. Potter's store on Monday afternoons. No one else was there on Mondays—Logan was gone off to play in the marching band, Donita was at choir, and Ricky Ray had his weekly social worker visit—so me and Murphy worked on little projects, just adding bits and pieces to the fort's décor. Me, I was trying to sew some curtains by hand. Sewing of any sort is not in my nature, but I just flat-out liked the idea of curtains.

"Dagblast it!" I yelled one Monday after I'd poked myself with my needle for the third time in under a minute. "I'm bleeding all over my material!"

"You need a thimble," Murphy said, "and maybe some sewing lessons."

I stuck my thumb in my mouth and sucked on it for a second. "I was in Girl Scouts for three weeks once, but I never did get my sewing badge."

"Did you get any badges?"

"Nope. I was the world's worst Girl Scout. All I ever wanted to do was go camping, but the whole time I was in it, all anybody ever talked about was cookies this and cookies that."

Murphy sprinkled some gold glitter over a rusty metal wastebasket Corinne had let her haul off from the dorm. She'd covered the whole thing with swirls of glue first, and now the glitter stuck to the twirly pattern.

"My mother wasn't the sort of person to sign me up for Girl Scouts," she told me, shaking the wastebasket so that the extra glitter fell off in a sparkling shower. "She didn't have much interest in organized activities of any kind. She thought life should be as spontaneous as possible."

She turned and fixed me with a serious look. "Do you miss your parents?"

The question took me by surprise. I wasn't too used to talking about my parents with anyone. You'd think the subject would come up more often with foster-care kids, but in my case it almost never did unless I was locked in conversation with a social worker. I didn't have a real dramatic story like some kids I knew.

"I never knew them to miss them," I said. "I wish I remembered my mama. In my mind, she has silver-blonde hair, but Granny Lane says that's not right, that Mama's hair is just like mine, regular old brown. But her eyes are brown and mine are blue. Granny Lane says my eyes must be from my daddy's side."

Murphy applied a few more squiggles of glue to her wastebasket, then leaned back on her heels. "If I tell you something, will you keep it to yourself?"

"Sure," I said nodding, excited that Murphy wanted to confide in me. "I'm real good at keeping secrets."

"There were a lot of bad things about my parents dying," she said. "But one of the worst things was that right before the car accident, my mother was teaching me how to fly. Only she died before I learned everything I needed to know."

"Your mother could fly a plane?"

Murphy looked at me for what seemed to be a long time. "No," she said slowly. "She could fly. In the air."

My hands started to tremble. This was the most bold-faced, outrageous thing anyone had ever said to me. It almost scared me to hear it.

"Well, it wasn't like she was born knowing how to fly," Murphy continued. "She learned it from some New Guinea tribesmen she and my father met when they were doing research. The entire tribe could fly like a flock of birds. The chief respected my parents, so he taught them how. Really, the most important thing is to have the special talisman."

"Talisman?"

"Like a good-luck charm. That's what my blue stone is. My mother gave it to me right before she died."

"Did it work?"

"Once, almost. I jumped off of my porch, and suddenly it was like I was floating in the air. I put out my arms, and I ended up landing about five feet away from where I would have naturally hit the ground."

She paused to sprinkle a little more glitter. Without looking at me, she asked, "You believe me, don't you?"

If I'd been in fourth grade, I would have believed every word a hundred percent because in fourth grade you still believe in things even though you say you don't. In fifth grade I would have called her a liar straight to her face. Nobody believes in anything in fifth grade, not even when you're sitting by your-self in your own room.

But in sixth grade—where nothing was magical, and nobody said anything anymore about hidden bedroom passageways that led to fairylands or being the long-lost daughter of a faraway king—to even whisper in secret that you could almost fly was opening yourself up to a lifetime of laughter and ridicule. It hardly seemed worth it. So for Murphy to make such a claim, well, I had to take it seriously.

"Sure," I said, doing my best to sound like I didn't have a doubt in the world. "Of course I believe you."

Murphy smiled. She stood and rubbed glitter from her hands. "I knew you would. It's nice to have someone to tell things to, isn't it?"

Then she came over and kneeled down beside me, picking up the edge of a curtain and running her finger over the crooked hem. "I think my mother would have taught me more, but she was sick a lot."

"What kind of sick?" I asked, picturing a pale woman lying in bed with a damp rag across her forehead. "Like the flu?"

"No. Nobody knew what was wrong with her," Murphy said, each word coming out careful, like she was weighing it in her mind before she spoke. "But some days she couldn't take care of me very well. Flying lessons were out of the question."

"Couldn't your daddy teach you?" I asked.

"He was gone a lot, doing research. Fortunately, I'm a very independent person. I can take care of myself."

She dropped the curtain and hopped back up. "Did you know I know how to bake a ham?" Now her voice was light, carefree as a butterfly. "And I can make potatoes six different ways."

She went back to her glitter, chattering away about how to double-bake a potato with butter and cheddar cheese. I picked up my needle and started hemming again, humming under my breath. Murphy told me secrets. Murphy was happy to have me to talk to. I couldn't help but smile, now that I knew for sure that me and Murphy were friends. Of course Murphy can fly, I told myself. Of course I believe her.

Chapter 10

One day, without saying a word to me about it, Murphy showed up at the fort with the *Book of Houses* and the *Book of People* in her backpack. "If it's okay with Maddie, I think we should all work on the books together," she told us. "It will help us think about the houses we might live in someday. We could also make up our own city and tell stories about it. That's something I've always wanted to do."

Donita walked over and took the books from Murphy. She leafed through the *Book of Houses*. "These the scrapbooks you and Ricky Ray used to work on all the time?" she asked me. "They're for pictures of houses?"

"And people," I told her, feeling nervous, worried

she might make fun of them.

"Well, y'all obviously been working hard," she said. She sounded like she approved. "That's the most houses I ever saw in one place."

She closed the book and looked at Murphy. "I don't know about making up a city, though. We already built a fort. Ain't that creative enough for you?"

"That's my point," Murphy said. "The fort is built, and now we need something else to do. We don't have to make up a city. That's just one idea for what we could do with the books."

Donita handed them back to her. "I'll cut out pictures of houses. Like I said, I don't know about no city."

"We'll be spontaneous about it," Murphy said. "We'll just do whatever comes to mind. If it's okay with Maddie, that is."

I looked around the room at each and every one of them, face by face. Donita had her practical look on, a look that made it clear she thought the rest of us needed her to keep our feet on the ground. Logan's expression went this way and that, like he wasn't sure someone signed up for Algebra I next year should be playing cut-outs—but if Murphy wanted him to, did he really have a choice? Ricky Ray's face was as eager as a puppy's.

Murphy was holding the books close to her chest. She looked at me solemnly, with the smallest of smiles, and I thought right then she knew how important those books were to me, and that she wouldn't ever let anything happen to them.

After a long minute I nodded my head. "It's okay with me," I said.

Logan went to his house and came back with scissors and copies of *Southern Living* and *Good Housekeeping*. "This is the best I can do right now," he said. "All the other stuff we have is *Sports Illustrated* and *National Geographic*."

That's how it became our routine, to meet at the fort and cut out pictures and put them in the books.

Now I figured we'd spend most of our time making up a city, just like Murphy wanted. But the day Ricky Ray cut out a picture of a modular home from the newspaper and stuck it into the book, making Donita laugh and say, "That thing ain't nothing but a gussied-up double-wide. Just a big hunk of junk by the side of the road," I couldn't help but tell the story of living with my Aunt Fonda, who was really one of Mr. Willis's cousin's daughters.

"If you don't count Granny Lane's trailer as a house, then the first house I ever lived in was a modular home," I said. I turned to Logan and Murphy and explained, "That's the kind of house you buy at a dealership, and they ship it to your empty yard on a flatbed trailer. But it wasn't a bad place to live at all."

I'd just turned eight when I moved down to Blountville to live with Fonda. Even back then I knew there were pluses and minuses to every situation. On the minus side of this one, I'd had to leave Granny Lane and Mr. Willis, the only family I'd ever known. On the plus side, I had my very own room for the first time in my life.

"It was on the far left side of the house," I told everyone, pointing to where my room would have been in Ricky Ray's picture. "And right outside the window was a black walnut tree. You could sell those walnuts unshelled for a ten cents a pound over at Blountville Herb and Metal."

"Was it a big room?" Ricky Ray asked. "Big as this fort?"

I shook my head. "If you spit across it, you'd better watch out, because that spit would bounce right back in your eye."

Fonda's girls, Peyton and Tiffany, had a bunk bed in the room across the hall from me. Ten-year-old twins, they were about the most glamorous girls I'd ever known. They liked giving their old things to me, torn dress-up clothes, junky tea party dishes, coloring books with almost all the pictures colored in. After only a month at Aunt Fonda's, I had that room of mine so done up with odds and ends, including a play oven and a small but real refrigerator without a cord, that I could stay in it all day, playing house. I could barely turn around in that room, but in my mind it was the size of a mansion.

Only problem was, I had that room done up a little too nice. When summer came around, Peyton and Tiffany started edging me out, telling me I could go sit on the top bunk all by myself, while they doodled and dawdled in my room, making up phony conversations like they were married and having dinner parties. "Oh, Justin is going to turn purple when he sees I burnt the roast," I remember Peyton exclaiming during one game of Dinner Party. "I reckon he'll want a divorce," Tiffany agreed.

"The kicker was," I concluded, "they liked that room so much, they decided I was in the way. They got talking to their mama, and the day after Labor Day I met my first social worker walking down Aunt Fonda's gravel drive."

"Social workers," Ricky Ray said, sighing. Everyone but Logan nodded glumly. "But I'm glad you got kicked out of your Aunt Fonda's so you could come over here."

"I had a lot of stops in between here and there," I reminded him. Before I could tick all the places off on my fingers, Ricky Ray counted them out for me. "Three homes in one year," he said. "The Grindstaffs, the Honeycutts, and the Fulks. And then Mrs. Estep's for a long stretch before coming to the Children's Home."

I couldn't help but think of my life at Mrs. Estep's as I watched Ricky Ray a few days later kneeling over an old copy of *Seventeen* magazine, clipping out a picture of a girl with pink hair and a dragon tattoo on her shoulder. You could tell he was serious about cutting her out exactly right. Ricky Ray did not take his role as a contributor to the books lightly, no sir.

"Now this girl, her name is Crystal, and once upon a time she had a little boy with blond hair," Ricky Ray said, taking one last snip. He held the paper girl at arm's length and admired his handiwork.

Rain tapped on the roof of the fort but didn't come in, a fact we were real proud of. It was the first week of October and the sky had been sending down rain steadily since Thursday, but here it was Saturday and not a drop had made it inside. Donita and Logan had taken plastic wrap and a staple gun to close the windows against the nonstop drizzle.

"What happened to the little boy?" Donita asked from where she was curled up in an old armchair with fluff coming out of its cushions. It was one of a bunch of chairs Logan had contributed from his parents' garage. Three of them were folding chairs, two were chairs that went with a dining-room table that Judge Parrish was using in his study, and one was the armchair where Donita sat. She had the *Book of Houses* in her lap and was pasting in a picture of a Williamsburg colonial.

"He ran away," Ricky Ray told her. "See, Crystal, his mama, was a princess, only she had been stolen by bad fairies when she was just a little girl. She missed her own folks real bad, but she didn't know what had become of them or where their castle was or anything. She just cried and cried about it. So her little boy, when he got big enough, decided to go find the castle that was his mama's true home."

"He was on a quest," Logan said from where he sat on a folding chair in the corner, leafing through an old copy of *Family Circle*.

Ricky Ray leaned back and considered this. "I guess that's what you might call it. He went off looking for something. Is that a quest?"

Logan nodded. "You got it."

"Then he was on a quest," Ricky Ray agreed. He turned to me and grinned. "You know what the boy's name was, Maddie?"

I shook my head. "Was it Ricky Ray?"

Ricky Ray looked at me like he couldn't believe I didn't know the right answer.

"No way," he said. "The boy's name was Randy. Why, it was Randy Nidiffer."

Chapter 11

Once, when Ricky Ray was four, his parents went to a party and didn't come back for two weeks. Every day while they were gone, Ricky Ray ate a peanut butter sandwich for breakfast, had another peanut butter sandwich for lunch, and then ate two peanut butter sandwiches for dinner.

If he hadn't run out of peanut butter and bread, he might have gone on living that way forever. It was when the manager of the Winn-Dixie store caught four-year-old Ricky Ray sitting in the middle of aisle five tearing into a loaf of Wonder bread, an open jar of Jif peanut butter by his side, that the Department of Social Services was called to investigate the situation. That's when Ricky Ray got put into foster care. He'd been officially recognized as a neglected child.

It meant something to Ricky Ray that Social Services took Randy Nidiffer away for the same reason they took him. When you're a foster-care child, you're always looking for kids whose stories are like your own. It makes you feel less lonely. Now, Randy's mama didn't leave him alone much, that's true. He used to say that his mama was usually home but she was hardly ever there. I think he meant she drank a lot.

"I got two little brothers, but they always stayed over at Mawmaw's, so they didn't get neglected so bad," Randy told me one afternoon when we were working on our books, cutting up the glossy inserts from Sunday's newspaper. "The State thought Mawmaw ought to take me in, too, but she disagreed with 'em."

"Why was that?" I asked, reaching over him to grab the Sears insert.

Randy gave me what he called his charm school grin. "Said I was too wild. Said she done got the little boys trained up right, but my mama let me get out of hand." He snipped around a picture of a lawn mower. "Just imagine. I was only six years old, and already I was purely ruined."

"You don't seem ruined to me," I told him. He didn't, either. He was the best artist I knew, and his hair shined like the sun had set in it. How could a boy like Randy be ruined?

"That's because you look at folks for what's good in their hearts. Mawmaw, mostly what she looks for is the black spots."

When I told this story in the fort, as a way of introducing the idea of Randy Nidiffer to everyone, Ricky Ray smiled. "You can't be ruined when you're six," he explained to Murphy, Logan, and Donita. "That's way too little. Randy Nidiffer wasn't ruined at all. His granny was wrong."

"Randy Nidiffer had freckles everywhere you could see," Ricky Ray told us, settling back into his story. "Which was a good thing, because freckles are nice. But it was a bad thing, too, because it made it easier for the bad fairies to see him."

"Were they glow-in-the-dark freckles?" Logan asked. I shot him a nasty look, and he rolled his eyes at me in return. But then he turned to Ricky Ray and said, "I mean, were they magic in any way?"

Ricky Ray shook his head. "He wasn't a magic boy. The fairies were magic, but Randy Nidiffer was just regular."

He walked over and took the *Book of Houses* from Donita, and then he walked to the middle of the room and kneeled on the floor and began flipping through its pages.

"Okay," Ricky Ray said, turning one page, then another, pointing to different houses. "Randy Nidiffer passed by this house and this house, and then he passed by this one. But when he came to this house," he said, pointing to a picture of an old-fashioned mansion in the style of a Halloween haunted house, "he stopped. There were spiders in the mailbox. That was a clue."

"What kind of clue was it, Ricky Ray?" Murphy asked from where she was sitting in the corner. She pulled her knees up to her chest and stared at him real hard.

"Well," Ricky Ray said, stretching out the word to give himself time to come up with an answer. "Well, Randy Nidiffer knew that bad fairies like spiders for pets. So there must have been some bad fairies who came to this house and left their spiders there when they went away. And this house was so big, it was the kind of house where a king and queen might live, too."

"Randy thought that's where his grandparents stayed," Donita said, pointing at the haunted house picture with her scissors.

Ricky Ray said, "Yeah, and he was right, too. Only he had to go and make sure, but he couldn't get past the spiders in the mailbox."

"So what did he do?" I asked. I could just see Randy Nidiffer with his hands on his hips, tapping his foot impatiently as he tried to come up with a solution to this problem.

Ricky Ray grinned. "He knocked the mailbox down. And then he stomped the spiders. And then he ran back to his house and got Princess Crystal and brought her home to the castle. The end."

We all clapped. It wasn't a bad story for a six-year-old boy to come up with.

Murphy had a somber expression on her face as we packed up the scissors and magazines for the afternoon. "I think Randy Nidiffer's grandmother was a spider," she said. "A spider disguised as an old woman. Spiders suck the blood out of things, right?"

Donita looked at her strangely. "Yeah, so do vampire bats. Maybe Randy Nidiffer's granny was Count Dracula."

"No, no," Murphy insisted. "That's the wrong story. The story of Randy Nidiffer's grandmother is the one where she spins a web and traps his little brothers, but Randy gets free."

"If you say so," Donita said. "She sounds like just another mean old lady to me."

That night in our room after lights-out, Murphy whispered, "Maddie, are you still awake?"

"Sure," I answered, turning toward the sound of her voice in the bed next to mine. "Are you okay?"

"Tell me about your grandmother and that old man," she said. "Tell me a funny story about things they used to do."

"Okay," I said. I propped myself up on my elbows. "But how come?"

Murphy pulled the sheets up to her neck. "It'll keep me from dreaming about spiders."

So I told her the story about the time Granny Lane and Mr. Willis decided to go to the church Halloween party as a horse, only they fought so hard about who'd be the head and who'd be the behind that they stopped talking to each other for a week and missed the party altogether.

When I finished, Murphy was fast asleep. I crept over to her bed and smoothed down her sheets and brushed a curl from her forehead. I would've bet she was used to her mama doing that for her every night. I would've bet she was missing home.

Chapter 12

For the first two months of her life as a citizen of the East Tennessee Children's Home, Murphy belonged to the fort and to us. If anyone else was trying to get her attention, hoping she'd turn around and look in their direction, they were just so many tree branches clicking against the window on a windy afternoon.

And then one day, this began to change.

The first time I noticed it was at lunch a few weeks after we'd finished building the fort. It was me, Murphy and Logan, all of us poking at our Tuna Melt Delights with our forks because there was a rumor going around that instead of tuna, the lunch ladies had chopped up gerbils and melted cheddar cheese over them. We didn't really believe it, but for a few minutes it was fun to pretend.

As we were busy poking and prodding our sandwiches, an eraser flew across the cafeteria and hit Murphy in the head. It was the kind of eraser that you stick on the end of your pencil, and the person who threw it was Brandon Sparks, the star soccer player of the sixth grade.

Murphy rubbed her head where she'd been hit, then picked up the eraser and examined it. "I've been bombed," she told us, then looked over at Brandon. "I think you lost this," she yelled at him.

I waited for Brandon to say something low-down and rude, but instead he called, "Then I guess I better come find it." The next thing we knew, he was standing next to Murphy with his hand stuck out. "Give it over, thank you very much."

Murphy folded her fingers over the eraser. "No way," she said. "Finders keepers. Besides, I have a lot of things I need to erase today."

They continued joking around like that for a few minutes, ending with Brandon's grand gesture of making a gift of the eraser to Murphy. The whole time he didn't say a word to me or Logan, or even act like we were alive.

Over the next few days I began to hear Murphy's name everywhere. I heard it as I was walking through the hallways or dressing out for gym, like it was part of a song everyone all the sudden knew the words to. "Her parents died in a car crash," kids told each other, their voices quiet and dramatic. "She's waiting for her aunt to come rescue her," they reported, "but she probably won't."

One day Olivia Woods picked Murphy for her team in PE. Olivia Woods was always a team captain, but she only picked three or four people for her team. After the special few were chosen, Olivia stepped back and let one of her followers, Jaycee Laws or Katha Coleman, pick out the rest. When Olivia called out Murphy's name, somebody actually gasped. Murphy walked over to Olivia's side like it was no big deal at all, like maybe she could fly and who cared what Olivia Woods thought. I knew this would make Olivia Woods like her even more. That was how the Olivia Woodses of the world operated, as far as I could tell.

"Olivia Woods keeps talking to me," Murphy told me one Monday afternoon when we were working at Potter's Used Auto Parts and Misc.

Supplies. We were going through shoe boxes filled with nuts and bolts and screws, sorting them out and storing them in plastic containers. Mr. Potter was up front, talking to a man about carburetors.

"Oh, yeah?" I asked, sifting through a pile of medium-sized bolts. "What about?"

"How I should come over to her house and eat dinner," Murphy said. "How her mother collects oriental carpets so you can't wear shoes inside. How she has a window in her ceiling and counts stars at night until she falls asleep."

"When does she tell you all this stuff?"

Murphy shrugged. "In math class. Between lunch and PE. On the way to the buses in the afternoon. She keeps slipping in conversations when I'm not looking."

I scraped at the rusty head of a screw with my fingernail. I hated Olivia Woods and wanted to be Olivia Woods' best friend all at the same time. I wanted her to leave Murphy alone. I wanted her to call me up and invite me over to eat pizza on her mama's fancy rugs.

"So what does it all mean, do you think?" I asked. "You think she wants to be friends with you?"

"Who knows?" Murphy said. "We're going to be partners for a math project. I'd rather do it with Logan, though. Sometimes Olivia acts like she's a pretty big ball of cheese."

"I've noticed," I said, and left it at that, even though my brain had already started buzzing with worries, like what if Olivia Woods stole Murphy away?

Mr. Potter walked into the back room, his hat on his head. "Just got a call about some parts from an old junker a man wants to sell me over near Hampton. It's on the other side of town, but I thought you children might like to ride along for a change of scenery. Don't know how much chance you got to get out and about, what with school and all your activities."

I glanced at Murphy, and she nodded. "Driving is one of my favorite pastimes," she told Mr. Potter as she started putting the lids back on boxes. That made Mr. Potter smile.

"Didn't know they let children your age drive, little gal," he said, returning a box of nuts and bolts to its place on the shelf. "You sure you can see all the way over the wheel?"

Murphy tossed her head. "Oh, you know what I mean. But watch out, I'm the worst backseat driver you ever met. I'm the sort of person who likes to give directions."

The inside of Mr. Potter's truck smelled like a mix of gasoline and peppermint. It made me think of Mr. Willis's truck, how it used to carry a whiff of wintergreen from the tobacco he liked to chew and spit into a plastic cup on the floorboard. "I swear, Virgil, that right there is the nastiest habit a man can have," Granny Lane would complain every time Mr. Willis spit out another brown stream into that cup. "It's worse than smoking, belching, and the public passing of gas all wrapped up together."

"And still all them women are crazy about me," Mr. Willis always said right back. "I got to spit tobacco just to get some peace and quiet."

"When I lived up on Roan Mountain, I rode around in a truck like this all the time," I told Mr. Potter as we drove down Elk Street on the way to Highway 19E to Hampton.

"Is that so? Well, for my money, you can't beat a Ford truck. Now my brother, Clinton, he had the misfortune of marrying a woman who couldn't abide a Ford truck. No sir, she came from a family of folk who didn't drive nothing if it didn't have the word *Chevrolet* on it in ten different places. Clinton was so in love, he traded in his Ford for a Chevy, and I can't tell you how many times over the years I had to go bail him out from some mess or another, that truck of his broken down on the side of the road."

"My father drove a Chevy truck to work," Murphy said. She said it like this was a fact she'd just remembered after a long time of forgetting. "A red one. He said that red trucks just rode better."

Mr. Potter shook his head. "Good thing I already like you as much as I do, little gal. Don't know about them Chevy trucks, now. But I do like the color red."

We pulled out onto 19E. I turned my head this way and that, catching sight of things I hadn't seen since I was eight years old. 19E is the road that goes from Elizabethton to Roan Mountain and back again, and I can't tell you how many times me and Granny Lane and Mr. Willis rode down it to get to the Elizabethton Wal-Mart. Saturdays and Sundays, you could be sure there'd be a caravan of shiny pickup trucks and rusty clunkers headed down from Roan Mountain, and on your way you'd pass cars from Boone and Cranberry, Mountain City and Stony Creek, all on their way to the Wal-Mart, just like you.

I snuggled down in my seat between Mr. Potter and Murphy, remembering. I used to get so excited smelling that popcorn smell that hit your nose the minute you walked in the store's front doors. And driving home we'd sing songs and cut up, and at Christmas time Mr. Willis would always buy all three of us Santa Claus hats and foot-long candy canes, and he'd sing "Deck the Halls" at the top of his lungs all the way back up the mountain.

"I always did like this road," I said out loud to Mr. Potter and Murphy. "I always liked where it took me."

Mr. Potter nodded. "I suspect that's the highest compliment you can give a road."

"That's the only road worth driving on," Murphy agreed.

Chapter 13

The problem with my curtains was they didn't look like curtains were supposed to—at least not like the ones you see in magazines, all crisp and fluttery at the same time. My curtains looked more like used handkerchiefs. Sometimes I'd pull the thread too tight, and a hem would pleat up into a yellow and white gingham accordion. Or I'd be concentrating so hard on adding a row of zigzag bric-a-brac, that somehow I'd manage to twist up the material like a pretzel.

But for all that, I was mighty glad to have something to do on Monday afternoons. Otherwise I'd have been stuck having to listen straight-on to nonstop talk about Olivia Woods's, house.

The first time Murphy came back to the Home after an afternoon spent with Olivia working on their math project, I hopped onto my bed, practically rubbing my hands together, I was so ready to hear about how horrible Olivia had been. "So was she twice as mean at home? Or only half?" I asked Murphy before she'd even had a chance to set her books down.

"She wasn't mean at all," Murphy said, slipping out of her jacket. "But that doesn't surprise me, really. I've seen it a million times."

"Seen what?"

Murphy flopped down on her bed and folded her arms behind her head. "A person changes from place to place. Like if you were in one house that had beautiful wallpaper and snow white carpets, you might sit up straighter or speak as properly as you could. But then if you went next door to a shabby, old house with no carpet and paint peeling off the walls, you'd feel entirely different. You might forget to close your mouth when you chewed your food or to wash your hands before dinner."

"So what's Olivia like when she's in her own house?"

"Like someone who looks at the moon through a window in her ceiling. It's the house, of course.

That house would make anyone a better person."

And from then on, that house was all Murphy wanted to talk about.

"You can tell someone with a very old soul designed Olivia's house," Murphy said one Monday afternoon. She was bent over a cardboard box that she was painting blue. "Someone who appreciates big spaces, lots of air."

"Why would an old soul appreciate big spaces? I'd think a soul would get tired of space after awhile," I remarked, biting off a length of thread. "In fact, you'd figure a soul might appreciate a closet, just something to stay inside of for awhile."

"Wrong," Murphy said, not bothering to look up from her box as she corrected me. "A soul needs air and light, and lots of it. Which is what Olivia's house has a million times over. It has three balconies on the inside, so you can see every downstairs room from the upstairs."

"I'd be careful about walking around in the dark, if you ever spend the night there."

"Maddie, do you not understand what I'm talking about here?" Murphy looked up and shook her head at me. "This house is nothing to joke around about. It's a fairy tale . . . it's poetry! Olivia's house is an actual poem made out of wood."

"Not to mention air and light," I added, making Murphy shake her head again and sigh.

I squinted my eyes at my curtains, like squinting might make the stitches straighten themselves out. If Murphy was going to fall in love with a house, how was I supposed to stop her? I wished I could build a house like a poem, a house that would make Murphy feel right at home, but dang if I could even make a pair of curtains that hung straight. Besides, in all her talk, I noticed Murphy hardly said a thing about Olivia. I couldn't care less if she fell in love with Olivia's house, as long as she didn't give two hoots about the girl who lived inside it.

I had other things to worry about, anyway, like what was I going to do about Ricky Ray, now that he'd been abandoned for the second time in his life.

It had been two days since I'd met Crystal Jenkins, Ricky Ray's mother, and I still hadn't gotten over it. She was about the last person on earth I'd ever expected to meet. I had this movie that showed in my head every time Ricky Ray mentioned her, where she was wearing a party dress and dancing farther and farther away from her little boy. Two weeks down the road, two months down the road, forever down the road. The idea that she might ever turn around and walk on back had never occurred to me.

But there we were, sitting across from each other, eating lunch at the Tres Chicas Café on Elk Street, Ricky Ray between us jabbing his spoon into his peanut butter and jelly sandwich like he held a longtime grudge against it.

I couldn't believe she'd ordered that peanut butter sandwich to begin with, but I'd sat right there as she'd pointed to the menu with a pudgy, nail-bitten finger and said to the waitress, "Peanut butter and jelly on white for the little boy. You know that's all they'll eat at his age."

Ricky Ray stared straight ahead, not saying a word.

"Ricky Ray, stop it," his mama said, pulling the spoon from between his fingers after he'd practically cracked his plate with it. "You're making me nervous. I'm nervous enough as it is."

There were a whole lot of things I'd had all

wrong about Crystal Jenkins. Clearly, she was too roly-poly for party dresses, and anything frilly or froo-froo wouldn't have been her style in the first place. Practically the only time her head came all the way out of her baby blue windbreaker with a race-car patch right over her heart was to order an egg salad sandwich. As soon as the waitress was gone, like a turtle, Crystal Jenkins's head popped right back down. It would have been hard to pull that kind of disappearing act in a slinky party dress.

"It sure surprised me when you showed up with Ricky Ray," Crystal Jenkins said to me after the waitress set down three glasses of iced tea on the table. "When he said he wanted to get permission to bring a friend, I figured it'd be somebody closer to his own age."

I shrugged. "Me and Ricky Ray have always been friends," I told her. "I don't see that age has all that much to do with it."

"I'm almost seven," Ricky Ray put in. "She ain't that much older than I am."

"Almost five years," I said, and he started to do the math on his fingers. I grabbed his hand.

"Believe me, it's five years. I'll be twelve in April. But it doesn't matter."

Ricky Ray pulled his hand back. "But I'll be seven in December," he said, and started counting again.

Crystal popped her head back out of her jacket. "Seven? Really?"

"Don't you know that?" Ricky Ray's eyes were open so wide I thought they might fall splat onto the table. "Don't you know how old I am?"

"Of course I know how old you are," she said, not sounding too sure. "I just can't believe how fast the years go. Boy, you sure are getting big."

Ricky Ray shrugged. "I told you, I'm almost seven."

I ripped open a sugar packet and dumped it in my tea. We'd been in the restaurant for about twenty minutes, but already it felt like the twelve months strung between one Christmas and another. When Ricky Ray had asked me to go to lunch with him and his mama, I pictured sitting at a table with somebody young with bright eyes and hair, someone who'd keep me laughing the whole time, like one of the models in the magazines that Ricky Ray was always calling Crystal. I'd spent the two days between the invitation and the lunch hardening myself to what I was sure would be Crystal Jenkins's charms. But an overload of charm wasn't one of Crystal's many problems.

"I tried to get your daddy to come," she told Ricky Ray through a mouthful of mushy egg salad. "But that good-for-nothing jerk wouldn't even try to get off work. I told him, 'Ain't neither one of us has seen little Ricky Ray in over a year, and you can't get off work.' Now if I'd told him I had a keg of beer back at my place, then he'd have gotten off work, you can count on it."

"That's okay," Ricky Ray said, staring at his sandwich. "I don't care."

Crystal put down her sandwich and pulled a pack of cigarettes from her pocket. "Can I smoke in here?" she asked a passing waitress, who shook her head no. Crystal turned back to us. "You pay half your wages in taxes, but the government don't let you smoke nowhere," she complained. "Those guys starting armies out in Idaho are on to something. I can't blame 'em a bit."

"Smoking's bad," Ricky Ray said. "You shouldn't smoke."

"Stress is what'll kill you," Crystal said, pointing at him with her cigarette pack. "I know a woman, ninety-three years old and still smoking. Never worried about a thing a day in her life. It's the stress what gets you, not the cigarettes."

"I'm sorry," I said. "But that doesn't make any sense."

"You'll understand in a few years, little girl. Believe me, it'll all come clear to you then."

Crystal stuffed her cigarettes back in her pocket and lowered her head into her jacket. "Are you cold?" I asked. "Because if you're cold, maybe you ought to get some hot tea instead of iced tea."

"I ain't cold," came out her muffled answer. Then she turned her turtle head toward Ricky. "They going to give you a birthday party over there? They ought to. Taxpayers' dollars are going to support that home. They ought to give little children birthday parties."

You ought to give a little child a birthday party, I thought. When I looked at Ricky Ray, he appeared to be shrinking in his seat. I wondered if he was thinking the same thing.

"You know, one of the reasons I wish your

no-account daddy would have come today is that we have something important to talk about," Crystal said after waving to the waitress for the check.

Ricky Ray sat up straight again, and I leaned toward Crystal. Had she come to take Ricky Ray home? The very thought made me feel shaky in my hands and knees.

"I was talking to Mrs. Weston over at the Children's Home," Crystal went on, "and, well, I think that if someone wants to adopt you, then they ought to let you be adopted. I'm on disability for my bad knee right now, and your daddy ain't going to take you, so maybe you ought to have a chance to be with a family that wants you."

I put my hand on Ricky Ray's shoulder. I wanted so bad for him not to cry. I just plain hated the thought of Crystal Jenkins going back home to tell everyone how her little boy bust out sobbing when she let him go.

But Ricky Ray's eyes got wide and filled with water, and the big, fat tears trickled down his cheeks. "I don't really like peanut butter all that much," he told his mama, his voice breaking with a sob. "So if you ever stop by to take me out for lunch again, maybe you could order me something else."

And then he took off like a shot, scattering a flock of ladies heading for their table and sending a waitress reeling back toward the kitchen, her tray going this way and that.

"You'd think she'd know how old I am," he yelled as I followed him out the door. He torpedoed up Allen Avenue toward the Home, and I had to sprint to keep up with him. "You'd think she'd know I don't like peanut butter sandwiches."

Then he pulled up short and turned to point at me. "You know I don't like peanut butter, Maddie. You wouldn't forget that."

"I never would," I promised him.

All the way home, all I could think about was how at least my mama made a clean break and didn't leave me hanging on the way Crystal did Ricky Ray. At least my mama had had the good sense to leave early and make it clear she was never coming back. Someone really ought to write a rule book, I thought. You know, *Proper Etiquette for Neglecting and Abandoning Your Child*. And rule 1 should be: If you're going, get out early and stay gone.

So there you have it. My mama did one thing right. Now if she'd only hung around long enough to show me how to sew a simple pair of curtains, I'd be all set, I told myself, ripping out the hem of my curtains for the millionth time, Murphy's chatter about Olivia's castle running swirling around me like a song I didn't want to hear but couldn't get out of my head.

Chapter 14

Logan pointed to a picture of a ranch house that someone had pasted into the book. The house was made of red brick, and part of its front was blocked from view by a stand of pines.

"Man, my grandparents' house was just like that," he said, jabbing hard at the picture a couple of times with his finger. "We'd have Sunday dinner over there every week. It was just over behind North American Rayon, off of Sycamore Shoals. Every Sunday as we were leaving, my grandfather would give me and Marcy a dollar. 'Buy yourself a gum ball,' he'd say."

You could tell it was real important for Logan that all of us knew about his granddaddy's after-dinner dollars. I thought that was interesting, since Logan's family seemed like the type that had a whole lot of money, and a dollar couldn't mean all that much to him. I remember once when Aunt Fonda lost a five-dollar bill, she spent the afternoon in a frantic search. She went so far as to unzip the sofa cushions looking for it. I couldn't imagine Mrs. Parrish doing much more than checking under a pillow or two before she shrugged her shoulders and went on with her life.

"He was really great," Logan continued, shaking his head like he couldn't believe how wonderful his granddaddy had been. "A great, great guy. Sometimes in the summers, before Granddaddy died, I'd stay over there at my grandparents' for a week. We'd work on Granddaddy's truck and go fishing down at the creek. Did you know I know how to tie thirteen different kinds of knots? Granddaddy taught me that."

Logan picked up the *Book of People* and flipped it open to the middle. "This is one I cut out," he said, pointing to a picture of a man and a boy wearing orange hunting vests and camouflage pants. "The man's a little young, but it made me think of Granddaddy."

Ricky Ray moved in closer to get a better look at

the picture. "Did you ever go camping?"

"No, though once I went on a trip with Granddaddy and Gram in a rented RV. That stands for recreational vehicle," he explained to Ricky Ray, not sounding the least bit know-it-all about it. "Mostly we hung around outside the house. Actually, once or twice we set up the tent in the backyard, if that counts as camping out."

"Sounds like camping out to me," Donita said, and Ricky Ray nodded in agreement. I expected Murphy to join in with some story about camping with her parents on a big research trip, but she didn't seem to be paying much attention. She was staring out the window, a faraway look on her face, like she was waiting for the moon to show up.

"I guess this picture reminds me a lot of Granddaddy because he really liked the outdoors," Logan said. "He worked outdoors practically all his life."

A smile broke over Logan's face, like he was about to tell us something good, but the sound of sticks crunching and leaves crackling made us all turn to the window. The woods were usually pretty quiet. The rustling of squirrels scampering over the leaves, a crow cawing, those were the only sounds that broke the air most afternoons. Crunching and cracking definitely meant something—or someone—was afoot.

Sure enough, Mrs. Parrish stood outside the fort, a plate wrapped in foil in her hands. She was wearing a smart, red plaid jacket, black slacks, and fashionable hiking boots. I'll say this for Mrs. Parrish, she always had a look.

"Hello there," she called through the door. "I had some leftover goodies from my book club and thought you children might enjoy them. I've been looking for an excuse to come out and meet everyone."

"All right!" Ricky Ray yelled and scampered out of the fort. Everyone followed him except Logan, who went back to looking at the ranch house pasted in the *Book of Houses*. I hung back a second, wondering if I should stay with him, but when Mrs. Parrish called, "Hello, Maddie. It's nice to see you. Introduce me to your friends," I didn't have any choice but to go.

It was clear to me something wasn't right between Logan and his mother. I'd told him once

I thought his mother was nice, and he'd said, "She's okay. She's good at going to meetings and volunteering at stuff."

"How's she at being your mama?" I'd asked.

Logan didn't answer at first. He bent over his magazine to cut out another picture for the books. Finally he looked up and said, "She'd be good at being my mom if I were someone else."

When Mrs. Parrish finished chatting to us about school and the weather, she handed Ricky Ray her nice tray of cookies. "Logan can bring the plate back when you're through," she said.

I thought it was strange how she didn't bother to stick her head inside of the fort just to give Logan a "Hey" before she went back to the house. Come to think of it, I couldn't recall either of Logan's parents coming inside and admiring all the hard work we'd done. It was like it was enough for them that Logan had finally participated in a normal activity by building the fort and making some friends. Maybe now that Mrs. Parrish had seen all of us together, she would check "Get L. some friends" off her list and go to work on persuading him to trade his trumpet for a football helmet.

Ricky Ray turned to go back into the fort, with Donita on his heels saying, "I might as well have that last chocolate chip one if no one else's gonna eat it."

I was about to follow Donita inside when Murphy grabbed my arm. "Listen, Maddie, I've got to go," she said in a half-whisper. "I want to go see if Corinne will drive me over to Olivia's."

"Why don't you just go over there after school tomorrow?"

"I need to do it now," she said, sounding impatient. "I'm the sort of person that when I need to do something, I can't wait around."

"Well, if you think Olivia Woods is such a big ball of cheese, I guess you ought to go over there then." I turned to go back inside the fort, feeling a buzz of irritation down to my toes. It was one thing for Murphy to go over to Olivia's to work on her math project. It was another thing for her to take off without any warning in the middle of an afternoon at the fort.

Murphy's grip on my arm grew tighter. "Sometimes when I'm in her house, I feel like I used to live there, a long time ago. I can't explain it, but that's how it feels to me."

She glanced back at the fort. "Listen, could you just say I forgot a book at school? That I'm going to see if Corinne will drive me over to pick it up?"

"You want me to lie?"

"Not everyone understands about houses," Murphy said, dropping my arm like it had caught on fire. "But I was sure you did."

She turned and started running toward the wooded path. "Oh, go ahead and do what you want; it doesn't matter," she called.

When I walked back into the fort, Logan, Donita, and Ricky Ray were sitting on the floor, the books in the center of the small circle they made. The *Book of Houses* was still open to the picture of the red brick ranch. Logan was threading a shoelace through the eyelets of his left sneaker.

"Logan showed us a granny knot, which is the easy one," Ricky Ray told me when I walked back inside the fort. "And a bowline knot, which is hard. And did you know his granddaddy was Lowell Fraley of Fraley's Feeds? That's where Logan got his hat."

Logan was concentrating on his shoelace. Donita looked up at me and said, "Logan helped his granddaddy build a room onto his house last year. Says it took them a lot longer to build that room than it did to build this fort. Logan helped him lay the brick for it."

"That's neat, Logan," I said, but he didn't say anything back. For the first time since we built the fort, I felt something tight in the air, like Murphy had broken a rule by leaving. "Hey," I said, trying to sound light-hearted. "Murphy just remembered she left a book at school that she needs tonight. She's hoping Corinne will give her a ride over there."

"Corinne's gonna give her a lecture about responsibility," Donita said. "That's one of her favorite ones, along with her lecture on the topic of lying."

I sat down in one of the folding chairs and looked at my feet. Then I looked over at Logan. "I spent three weeks at Girl Scouts once before they kicked me out, so I can do a square knot. Probably a thousand times better than you can."

A grin fought its way onto Logan's face. "Oh, yeah? Why'd they kick you out of Girl Scouts then?"

"Dress code violation. I wore my rodeo belt buckle with my uniform; said it was a real big badge."

"Maddie, not really!" Ricky Ray cried. "You really didn't get kicked out of Girl Scouts, did you?

"Maybe I didn't," I admitted. "Maybe I just quit out of pure boredom. But I still can tie a square knot. My granny taught me."

We messed around awhile tying knots and telling dumb jokes, and the whole time all I could think was Murphy shouldn't have left that way. That's one thing I learned from Granny Lane and Mr. Willis. It's not polite to stop listening right in the middle of a story, especially when someone's trying to tell you something important.

Chapter 15

The fort was starting to fill up with all kinds of stuff, the way I suspect any house will do once you've lived it in awhile. There were the chairs that Logan had brought up from his house, always pushed here and there, never in the same spot two days in a row. Donita had gotten permission to take a carpet remnant from backstage at the school auditorium, and we'd laid it out in the middle of the room, careful not to cross its primrose border with muddy feet.

The north wall of the fort was filling up with pictures we'd pulled out of magazines and taped to it. Everybody had his or her own specialty. I had taken to cutting out pictures of pictures, so that my little corner of the north wall was like a miniature art gallery. I had a tiny blue Picasso painting and a picture of a framed Norman Rockwell I was real proud of.

Ricky Ray liked frogs, and Logan tore out ads for junk food because he claimed his mama was always on a diet and never had anything fun to eat in the house. Donita had different moods when it came to taping pictures on the wall. For awhile she was putting up real fancy furniture, and then she got on a famous people kick. Lately she'd been in a sports car mood.

Murphy always cut out words. *Enchanted. Allure. Soar.*

We had boxes for our stuff, the blue box for the books, and a box Murphy had painted blue with yellow flowers to hold my curtains with the halfway-sewn hems. There was Murphy's gold trash can filled to the brim with little scraps of paper.

Some days the fort filled up with other stuff, too. If someone did poorly on a test or had gotten yelled at by a teacher, then a corner would fill up with that person's sadness for the afternoon. When one of us came in with an A math quiz to our credit or a good day on the soccer field, the walls of the fort seemed to scoop up the joy and spread it around.

One afternoon the fort got so filled up with Ricky Ray's knock knock jokes, I thought if the walls didn't explode, I surely would. A six-year-old, even one who's almost seven, will knock knock joke you to death if you're not careful.

"Knock knock!" Ricky Ray yelled from where he was lying on the middle of the carpet. He was wearing the red and white scarf I'd bought him at Wal-Mart and looking mighty smart. He sounded cheerful as always, like that lunch with his mama had never occurred. But one afternoon when he was cutting out a picture for the *Book of People,* he pointed to the blonde-haired model and said, "Now this girl, her name is Amy, and she's a famous movie star."

Don't ask me why, but that made me sadder than I'd been in a long time.

"Knock knock!" he called out again, not letting us pretend we didn't hear him.

"Who's there?" Donita, me and Logan asked in a chorus, our voices dragging down low to the floorboards.

"Banana!"

"Oh, man," Donita groaned. "Not this one again. Ricky Ray, can't you get a book out of the library, figure out some new jokes?"

"Just say it, Donita!" Ricky Ray called out.

Donita sighed. "Banana who?"

"Banana banana."

"You're killing me, Ricky Ray," Logan said from the armchair. "Please, could we get this over with?"

"Okay," Ricky Ray said. "Orange you glad I'm not a banana?" He broke up in a fit of giggles and rolled around on the ground. "Okay," he said, rolling into a sitting position and catching his breath. "I've got another one. Knock knock!"

Logan, Donita, and me all looked at each other and shook our heads. "Who's there?" we answered.

I could tell you who wasn't there, and that was Murphy. It had been a week since she'd been up to the fort. The math project she had been working on with Olivia, a report on the subject of infinity, was due on Friday, so they'd been working on it every day after school. "I guess that could take an awful long time," I'd joked when she'd told me about it.

"Don't confuse infinity with eternity," she'd told me, all serious. "It's mathematically unsound."

I had two thoughts when she finally showed up later that afternoon. The first one was it had seemed like an infinite number of days since Murphy had last been at the fort. The second one was *Thank goodness.* Now Murphy could take her turn answering those dagblasted knock knock jokes.

Sure enough, Ricky Ray was the first one to greet her. "Knock-knock, Murphy!"

"Who's there?" she asked, still standing in the doorway.

"What's black and white and red all over?" Ricky Ray asked her.

"That's not a knock knock joke, Ricky Ray," Logan said. "That's a black and white and red joke."

"Oh," said Ricky Ray, looking confused. "Well, the answer is a zebra with diaper rash."

"I don't know why that can't be a knock knock joke," Murphy said. "Is there a rule that all knock knock jokes have to be exactly the same?"

Donita buried her head in her hands. "Oh, man, here we go again. Madam Weird is back."

"I think any kind of joke could be a knock knock joke," Ricky Ray said, and he was the only one who spoke. Now, instead of jokes, the fort was filled with an uneasy feeling. "What?" Murphy asked, turning around to look at everyone. "Why's it so quiet all of a sudden?"

Logan shrugged. "No reason. Ricky Ray just ran out of knock knock jokes, I guess."

Murphy began pacing the room, her mouth pulled into a tight frown. I wished I could explain to her that you just can't abandon people for a week and expect them to take you back with open arms. Especially not a bunch of abandoned and neglected kids. We're real sensitive to it.

After a few minutes of pacing, Murphy broke into the circle and picked up the *Book of Houses,* which she shoved into Donita's hands. "It's your turn to tell a story, Donita. So quit being mad at me and start talking."

Donita took the book from Murphy, her expression moving from irritation to uncertainty and back again. But she began turning pages, and when she stopped turning pages, she started talking.

Chapter 16

I stopped talking to the world exactly one week before I arrived at the East Tennessee Children's Home. That's when Mrs. Estep decided she didn't want to be a foster-parent anymore, no matter how much the monthly checks from the state of Tennessee improved her financial picture.

"What good does it do me to get a check from the state if them children are stealing from me?" I overheard her complain to her best friend, Mary Gaye Gaskins, over glasses of diet cola in Mrs. Estep's spotless kitchen. I'd been coming down the hallway to tell Mrs. Estep we needed to take a trip to the laundromat if she expected me to get dressed for school in the morning. When I heard her say that about state checks and children stealing,

I stopped dead in my tracks. My arms and legs felt shot full of electricity. She couldn't mean me and Randy, could she?

She most certainly could.

"I feel sorry for the girl," Mrs. Estep continued to her friend. "It's that boy's influence, I don't doubt that for a minute. Why, he's in trouble over at that school every other day. Tardy for class, stealing some child's pencil, not doing his homework."

"I don't know how you put up with it," Mrs. Gaskins said. "I've always said you were one of God's angels, taking these children in the way you do. And then they rob you blind."

I stood frozen to the carpet. Half of me wanted to rush into the kitchen and beg for forgiveness, and the other half of me was ready to run out the front door, never to darken the entrance to Mrs. Estep's house again.

The only thing was, I hadn't stolen anything from anyone.

Mrs. Estep sighed in the kitchen. "What breaks my heart is, I'd been saving that cash to take James and Ronnie to Bristol to do some clothes shopping.

Seems like so much of the money around here goes to children who ain't even blood kin to us. But James and Ronnie don't ever complain about it."

James and Ronnie were Mrs. Estep's sons. Nine and ten, neither of them had the least bit of interest in clothes or in anything besides television wrestling and firing off their BB guns at the neighborhood squirrels. If they had any idea a shopping trip to Bristol was in the works, they'd probably hightail it to the hills with their guns and a portable TV in hand.

When the front door opened and James and Ronnie themselves bolted inside, a plastic shopping bag dangling from Ronnie's wrist, I quick made my way back down the hallway. I didn't want them to know I'd been listening to their mama's conversation. I heard them turn on the TV in the front room, and then the sounds of them wrestling over something and shouting, "Give me that!" flew through the air. It didn't take me long to figure out what was going on.

"What did y'all get?" I asked casually, leaning over the back of an easy chair. "It looks to me like you been out to the mall."

James held up several cartridges. "Video games.

This one's called "Mortal Victory." I'm about to set it up if old fart-breath over here would let me handle it."

Ronnie lunged for the game, and the two fell to the ground in another battle.

I waited until they were done fighting before I said anything else. "So where did you get the money for it?"

"Uncle Pete," James said.

"Collected some cans," Ronnie said at exactly the same time.

"Well, it's always nice to have some extra cash," I told them.

James and Ronnie looked confused. Then they smiled, thinking they had gotten one over on me. I left the room, my mind in a jumble.

I didn't know what to do first: go tell Mrs. Estep that it was her own children, not me and Randy, who had stolen her money, or find Randy so we could have a laugh over the whole situation. I decided to go tell Randy.

"You might as well start packing your bags," he said after I had finished. "We'll be out of here by tomorrow."

"What do you mean? All we have to do is tell Mrs. Estep what really happened. It's obvious those boys stole the money and bought themselves new video games."

We were sitting on the carpet of the room Randy shared with James and Ronnie. Randy had a sketchbook in his lap. He turned it to a fresh page.

"Let's map this one out, okay? You and me, we're over here," he said, drawing two Xs and circling them. "And James and Ronnie, they're over there."

He drew two more Xs on the other side of the page and circled them. "Now here's Mrs. Estep," he said. With a few quick strokes of his pencil, Randy made a perfect study of our foster-care mother. She sat at the bottom of the page, holding her hands over her heart and looking adoringly toward her two boys.

"Now it don't matter to Mrs. Estep if we're no good or not," Randy continued, looking up at me. "She didn't raise us and she can't be blamed for our bad behavior, though I've heard her take credit for your good grades a time or two.

"On the other hand, she did raise them two

boys, and besides that, she's pretty sure they hung the moon, not to mention the stars. You tell her they stole the money she was saving to buy them some new BVDs and tube socks, and she'll probably call the police and have 'em arrest you for maligning her boys' characters."

"But if I don't tell her, she's going to get rid of us and say we're thieves."

"Honey, she's going to get rid of us and say we robbed her no matter what you do."

I couldn't believe it. Mrs. Theresa Estep was no saint, and she hadn't impressed me with the overall quality of her care, but she wasn't a mean woman to my knowledge. She wasn't even all that unreasonable, unless the subject was her boys. Besides, Randy had been there for two years and I'd been there over a year and a half, and that had to count for something.

"I'm going to talk to her," I told Randy, standing up.

"Suit yourself," Randy said. "Like I said, it won't make no difference one way or another." He drew a mushroom cloud over the circle that held the two of us together. "Mrs. Estep can't afford to think ill of them boys of hers. They're all she has. Us—she can think the worst of us. It won't cost her a dime."

I stomped down the hallway to the kitchen and demanded that Mrs. Estep face the truth: her boys were the only thieves in that house. As soon as I spoke, I saw her face close to my words like a plant at nightfall, and then it bloomed again in rage.

"Why, I ought to slap your face," she hissed at me through clenched teeth. "You better go get your things, missy. I'll have Social Services over here to fetch you and that juvenile delinquent in there directly."

No one could come pick us up until the next day. By then, my eyes were so swollen from crying I could barely see out of them. "I demand a trial!" I screamed as soon as the grim-looking social worker appeared at the door.

She grabbed me by the wrist. "You hush up now, young lady. You're in enough trouble as it is."

So I hushed. And I stayed hushed all the way over to the halfway house where they put me and Randy until they found new placements for us, and I stayed hushed on the trip to the East Tennessee

Children's Home in Elizabethton, my sorry-looking Barbie suitcase by my side, an old Raggedy Ann doll stuffed inside it, and Randy Nidiffer's grandmother's address in my pocket.

What was the use of talking if no one was willing to listen to the truth? And why would I talk to people who didn't understand you don't just tear two kids apart like a sheet of paper. Me and Randy were family. I was all he had and he was all I had. We had each other, and we had the books. And nobody in the world cared. So why bother to say a word to anyone?

I didn't intend to say a word to Donita when I first met her, that was for sure. If I was the quietest person in our room, she was the loudest, cutting up with Kandy and giving Corinne a hard time in a joking sort of way—like why didn't Corinne ever take us out to dinner at some fancy restaurant instead of making us eat the horrible dining-hall food? That first night at dinner, Donita'd described five different business plans she had for getting rich before she turned twenty-five, and you could tell by the confidence in her tone that she was sure she'd be successful one way or another. There was no way on earth someone like Donita could ever understand what I'd been through.

"You sure don't talk much," Donita said to me after I'd been there for a couple of days. She'd been giving me a tour of the Home, showing me all of those mismatched buildings.

"I hate to tell you, but Corinne likes folks to talk." Donita said. "You don't talk, she's going to send you to this therapist from our church, Dr. Pender. He does Bible therapy, quotes you the Psalms, reads Proverbs. It's like getting an extra dose of church-going every week."

I looked at her. She sounded like she knew a lot about it.

"Yeah, I went to see Dr. Pender," she said, reading my expression. "Most people here do. Bunch of crazy kids running around here. I ain't crazy, but I come from a crazy situation."

I didn't say a word. This is how I discovered that sometimes if you're real quiet, people will tell you stories that they might not tell you otherwise.

Donita led me to a spot of grass beside a row of newly sprouted seedlings. "Our dorm planted those flowers," she said, sitting down. "Me, I love sunflower seeds, so Corinne thought it'd be nice if we planted sunflower plants. Maybe she's just trying to save some money on snacks, though; I don't know."

She lay back on the grass, her arms crossed behind her head. "By the way, the food here is real bad. Lotta good things about this place, but the food ain't one of them. Now my mama, she could cook. That's what I miss most about things, my mama's cooking. You'd come home from playing outside sometimes, and the house would just smell so good, you would not believe it. Biscuits and gravy, that was my favorite. My sister, Rita, she liked her a good piece of ham and a bowl full of butter beans, and my brother, Russell, he liked pinto beans."

I leaned back on my elbows and looked up at the sky. I used to get pintos and corn bread when Granny Lane felt rich and took us to dinner at the K&W Cafeteria. I took in a deep breath and breathed out more quiet.

"Where we used to live, it was a real nice house," Donita told me, pulling up a handful of grass and throwing it toward the garden. "Painted white, fresh, right when we moved in. It was me and Mama, Rita, and Russell, and out back we kept a nice garden. Grew everything in it: beans, tomatoes, squash, lettuce when it got a little cooler. Russell grew sunflowers, too, just like here."

Donita propped herself up on her elbows. "I think about that garden every time it's my turn to come over here and do the watering. Think we ought to put a scarecrow up to keep the birds out. Russell made a scarecrow for our garden. Took Mama's old, wore-out gardening hat and stuck to the end of a rake. Then he got some of my cousin's overalls and stuffed them overalls with hay, and he tied pie pans to the overalls. It was the craziest thing. Made Mama laugh and laugh."

It seemed to me that for every word I didn't say, Donita said five. She reminded me of Randy, who would start telling you a story the second you walked into the room, no matter if it was first thing in the morning or the last thing at the end of the day.

"Feel free to add a word here and there," Donita said, reading my thoughts again. "If you got any questions or anything."

I shook my head. I didn't have any questions.

"You like videos? We rent a lot of videos on weekends. Only G-rated ones, though. They're real religious here. It's okay if you ain't. Nobody's gonna force you to believe anything you don't want to. My mama, she was religious, but not as religious as some. Some folks on our street spent every free moment at church. Mama spent all her free time in the garden. Russell, too. He loved the outside. He was real special."

I turned and studied Donita's face. She was smiling at her memories, but it was the sort of smile that you might call brave, like it was working extra hard to stay on her face.

That's when I said my first words in seven days. "What happened to Russell?"

Donita stared straight ahead. "You think nine is too young to get real sick, but it ain't."

Then she turned to me. "You should have seen his room in that house. He painted it himself. He was a real good painter. You never would've believed how good that room looked."

Chapter 17

That's exactly how Donita told her story in the fort that day. She talked about her house and Russell's paintings and how Russell was in the hospital for three months before he died.

"Leukemia," Donita told us. "That's what he had. He was real brave about it, though. He said mostly he was sad about not having more time to paint his pictures. That's what he loved doing best of all."

Donita traced her finger along a picture of a small, white house with a flower garden blooming beside the front walk.

"On one wall of his room, he painted a scarecrow, just like the one in the garden," she said, staring hard at that picture. "And on another wall, he painted a row of sunflowers and a big fat sun hanging over 'em. That was my favorite. And on the door, he painted a picture of our entire family, me and Mama, Russell and Rita, all dressed up like Christmas."

Then she looked over to Murphy. "Bet you didn't know I was going to tell such a sad story. You probably wouldn't have asked if you'd known."

"I wish I could see those paintings," Murphy said to her.

"Well, I'll be going back there one of these days to see 'em again myself. Mama's still in that house, and Rita's living with a family not three blocks away. Just as soon as Mama can get Russell's medical bills paid off, she won't have to work so much. And then she can take care of us better. That's what happened, case you were wondering. Rita started a fire on the stove one night when Mama was working third shift. Social Services got called in, said Mama wasn't fit to raise no children if she wasn't ever home."

Donita picked up a magazine and flipped through the pages without really looking at them. "I never saw anything like that fire," she said after a minute. "It started out this tiny little flame you could probably spit on and put out, except it just sort of exploded before Rita knew what to do about it. Rita, she was all upset about ruining Mama's kitchen, but me, all I could think about was that Russell would've loved to have seen that fire."

"He wouldn't mind your house burning down?" Ricky Ray asked.

"Nah, that ain't what I mean," Donita told him. "He just loved excitement. Loved big, dramatic things, and there ain't nothing more dramatic than a fire. If you hung around with Russell, you started seeing the excitement in everything. He could find it, boy. He'd find it, he'd study it, and then he'd paint it."

"He sounds like he was a born artist," Murphy said. "You can always tell."

"Yeah," Donita said, nodding. "Yeah, I guess he was."

I couldn't tell if Donita was softening to Murphy or not. Sometimes telling a sad story can make you feel more open to other people, but Donita was stubborn. It might take more than Murphy wanting to see Russell's paintings to make Donita like her again.

Murphy turned around slowly, examining the

walls. "We ought to paint a mural in here," she said. "I've been thinking for awhile we ought to do something more in here to give it more of a feeling."

"What kind of feeling?" Logan asked, giving Murphy one of those googly-eyed looks he hadn't had much time to practice on her lately. "How can a fort have feelings?"

"Any place can have a feeling to it," Murphy said, beginning to pace. "The library at school has a different feeling than the Elizabethton library, right? My dorm room feels a lot different from my old bedroom."

"My old bedroom had brown carpet in it," Ricky Ray said. "It felt a lot different from the floors at the Home."

"That's not quite what I mean," Murphy said, stopping by the door and poking her head out for a second. "But imagine if we had wall-to-wall carpet in here. A soft, white carpet and big, silky pillows you could lean back against. You'd feel like you were in an ancient story, "Aladdin and the Magic Lamp," something like that."

"This fort's fine the way it is," Donita said. But then her voice softened. "Though I suppose a mural might be nice. Maybe some sunflowers on it."

"And a scarecrow," Ricky Ray added. "I like scarecrows."

Murphy turned around and faced us. "Okay, it's my turn to tell a story. I've been trying to think up a good one for awhile, and I think I've almost got it." She turned to Ricky Ray. "I'll need a helper, though."

Ricky Ray nodded. "I'm good at helping."

Murphy settled herself in front of the easy chair and patted the space beside her where she wanted Ricky Ray to sit down. Then she pulled a folded manila envelope from her back pocket and opened the clasp. Ricky Ray brought her the *Book of Houses*, and then sat down beside her chair, posture-perfect and ready to be of assistance.

"So once upon a time there was a castle in the middle of a forest," she began, pulling a picture of a castle made of crumbling stone out the envelope. She handed the picture to Ricky Ray, who ran a glue stick over its back, then stuck it into the book. She shook the envelope onto her lap and out fluttered a few trees. "That's the forest," she told Ricky Ray. "Paste it in next to the castle."

She plucked a paper chair from the pile of pictures on her lap. "This is the throne upon which sat
the queen. The queen was a sad queen, and a mean
one, too. Her husband the king had died only a few
months before. Ever since his death the queen had
been a cruel ruler. She never listened to the king's
wisest advisor, a young woman named . . ."

And here Murphy looked up and grinned. "A
young woman named Bonita."

Donita shook her head, like she couldn't believe
such foolishness, but a smile broke through to her
lips all the same.

"Nor would the queen let the king's court jester,
Logarth, keep the court amused anymore. She had
no time for silly jokes."

"Oh, man," Logan groaned, and Ricky Ray
giggled.

"Even worse, the queen no longer allowed the
court artist, Maddelina, come paint magic pictures
for the court's delight, and she had banned everyone's favorite puppy, Micky May, from the castle."

"I'm a puppy?" Ricky Ray asked gleefully. He
barked a few times for good measure, but Donita
shushed him.

"Go on," she told Murphy, pulling her chair a little closer to where Murphy sat.

Murphy handed Ricky Ray a picture of a wall with a small window placed in the upper right-hand corner. "One morning, a red bird appeared at the window next to the queen's throne. 'I will bring you three gifts,' the bird told the queen. 'One each morning for the next three mornings. Each gift will last into forever, and you will never feel lonely or sad again.'"

Ricky Ray had finished pasting the picture of the wall into the book. When he turned the page, he let out a gasp. "This is the last page! The book is almost over!"

"We can get a new book," Logan assured him. "I'll get my mom to buy me one."

Murphy leaned over and looked at the book, then looked down at the pictures that remained in her lap. "I think we have enough room for the rest of the story," she said.

"Well, keep telling it then," I said. It was like I was caught in a spell, like I was sitting right next to the queen waiting for the bird to return.

Murphy smiled. "Okay, okay. Let's see," she

said, then pulled out a picture of a piano. "The next morning the bird came to the window and whistled a beautiful song to the queen. 'This song is now yours,' the bird said. 'Whenever you hum it, you will feel great happiness.' The queen hummed a few notes, and sure enough, she felt wonderful. She couldn't wait until the bird came back the next morning."

"I hope the bird brings her some candy," Ricky Ray said, taking the piano from Murphy and pasting it into the book.

"No, the bird brought the queen something even better," Murphy said. "When he came back the next day, he whispered a beautiful poem into her ear. She memorized it immediately, and whenever she felt the least bit sad, she said a few lines of the poem under her breath, and she immediately felt as though she were running along a beautiful beach, blue skies stretching over her head."

Murphy handed Ricky Ray a picture of a bookcase. She looked up and smiled. "That was the closest thing I could figure out for a poem," she said. "Poems come in books, right?"

"So what did the bird bring the third day?"

I asked, impatient for Murphy to get on with it.

Murphy looked down at her hands and shook her head. "I still haven't figured that part out yet," she admitted. Everybody groaned.

"Girl, you can't be starting a story and not have the end to it," Donita complained. "You better think hard tonight and come back tomorrow with something good."

We packed up our stuff, and Donita, Murphy, Ricky Ray, and I began our hike back to the Home. I was quiet, thinking about Murphy's story: what it meant, how it would end.

"Hey, Murphy," Ricky Ray said, as we turned down Dewey Payne Road, "are you the queen in your story? Is that supposed to be you?"

"No way," she said. "I'm not the queen type."

I looked at her, wondering about that. She was bossy enough sometimes to be a queen, and she was pretty like a queen in a fairy tale would be. But I knew Murphy well enough by then to know she wasn't the queen in her story.

No, Murphy could fly. Murphy was the red bird.

Chapter 18

I thought about Murphy's story all the next morning, trying to come up with a good ending for it. I knew that the third gift wouldn't be the end. There had to be something that came after, something that made you think everything was ruined until something or someone appeared to make everything right again.

I wasn't very good at fairy tales, though. Granny Lane never told me any. She liked her stories real-funny or real-sad. She never much went in for make-believe.

"Maybe the bird's going to give the queen a bottle filled with water from the fountain of youth," I told Logan and Donita at lunch. "So that she'll live forever."

"Too boring," Donita said, tearing the crust off her grilled cheese sandwich. "It's got to be something with a little more spark to it than that."

"Why don't you ask her yourself," Logan said, nodding toward the cafeteria entrance. Murphy hurried through the doors, holding something close to her chest. I waved to her, but she was headed for Olivia Woods's, table and didn't notice.

Donita shook her head. "Murphy's going to be sorry she ever got mixed up with that crowd, that's my prediction," she said, taking a bite of her sandwich. "They're mean as a pack of jackals."

I watched as Murphy sat down next to Olivia Woods. She smiled at everyone and chatted for a minute, leaning over once to touch Olivia on the arm. Katha Coleman and Jaycee Laws gave her some sniffy looks, but Murphy ignored them. She said something to Olivia and placed a black and white speckled notebook on the table.

That's when I knew what happened next in Murphy's story.

"The bird brings the queen a magic book," I said, standing up slowly.

"Are you okay, Maddie?" Logan asked. "Maybe

you ought to sit down and eat something."

By the time I reached Olivia's table, she was gingerly fingering the black speckled cover as though it might have something contagious on it. Cautiously, she began to leaf through the pages.

Then, to my everlasting surprise, Olivia Woods smiled.

It was an honest-to-goodness smile, not a smirk, not a sneer, not a grimace. I suddenly saw how she must have looked when she was six or seven, before she became the sort of person who made kids miserable because they'd bought the wrong brand of tennis shoes. It was like everything good that had gone into the *Book of Houses*—the afternoons spent in the fort making jokes and cutting up, the dreams of the day we'd have houses of our own with real families in them, the feeling that maybe we *were* a real family, just sitting there and telling each other stories—it was like all of that got under Olivia Woods' skin for a minute and made her soft and new as a spring morning.

But only for a minute.

"What is this, Murphy?" Katha Coleman exclaimed, squinching up her nose as she looked over

Olivia's shoulder. "It's really weird."

"It's something I've been doing with some friends," Murphy said. "It's like a story we've written, a story made up of a hundred tiny stories."

"I don't get it," Olivia said, her face gone blank, like a switch had been flipped off inside her. "You cut out pictures of houses? I mean, why?"

"They're houses we might want to live in someday." Murphy was talking fast, like she was trying to run after the other Olivia, the one who for a shining moment had understood exactly what the books were about. "We talk about them and make up stories about them. It's wonderful."

"Sure, if you're, like, eight years old or something." Olivia looked over at Katha and shook her head, like she couldn't believe what a baby Murphy was. "I mean, isn't this a little . . . immature or something? Cutting pictures out of magazines?"

"I don't know," Murphy said, her cheeks reddening. "I don't really think so. Actually, I thought you might like to do it, too, sometime. It's like making wishes, if you think about it."

A small ringing sound in my ears was growing louder by the second. I wanted so bad to snatch that book from the table and run as far away as I could, but I stood there, frozen as winter, not able to budge an inch.

"Oh, come on, Murphy! What's next? You're going to invite me over to play paper dolls?" Olivia said.

Katha leaned over to pull the book closer so she could find something to make fun of, too, and her arm knocked over someone's Coke. The dark liquid seeped into the pages, turning the edges black.

"Oops!" she said cheerfully. "Sorry about that, Murphy!"

Two seconds later, Brandon Sparks swooped down on the table and grabbed the book. "I'll save it!" he cried. "I'll save Murphy's book!" Then he tossed it to Jason Breem, yelling, "Speed dry!"

Jason shook the book out over his head so that a few of the pictures came unstuck and rained down on his hair. "What is this thing?" he yelled out so loud everyone in the cafeteria could hear him. "A recycling bin?"

Hands were waving in the air. "Here! Throw it here!" voices called. Olivia and Katha held their stomachs, like it hurt to laugh as hard as they were laughing. I looked around at Logan and Donita. They were both standing, yelling for everyone to put the *Book of Houses* down, to give it back, but one of Brandon's friends stood in front of them, his arms out like a guard who wouldn't let them pass.

Murphy sat as still as stone as the book flew from hand to outstretched hand. I couldn't move for what seemed like years, and then I turned and walked away.

I didn't ever want to see that book again.

Chapter 19

I couldn't bring myself to go to JM practice that afternoon. I didn't want to see Logan or anybody else for that matter. I tucked my head down into my jacket and pushed my way to the bus line. When I felt a hand on my arm, I shrugged it off, ready to shove an elbow hard into a rib cage if I had to.

Murphy dug her fingers into my arm and dragged me over to the end of the bus line, where the bus to Snob Hill stood hissing out gray smoke. "You know, I don't much care to go anywhere with you right now," I told her, trying to pry her hand from my arm.

"I know that," Murphy said, not turning around to look at me. "Don't you think I know that?"

I rolled my eyes, but I followed her up the steps and to the last row of seats. "Don't expect me to sit with you," I said, taking the seat in front of her, "because I sure don't have anything to say to you."

After the bus let us off, I trudged behind Murphy through Logan's backyard to the fort. The air smelled just right that afternoon, just the way the air two days before Halloween was supposed to smell, rich with leaves and dirt and smoke from the leaves people weren't allowed to burn, but always did.

By the time we reached the fort, the sky was already beginning to dim, and we wouldn't have long before we needed to turn around to get back to the Home for supper. As soon as we got inside, Murphy flung herself into the armchair and let her arms and legs flop out.

"Home sweet home!" she said, trying to sound cheerful. I gave her a long look and a big mess of silence.

"Maddie, I'm sorry about the book. Things didn't go the way I'd planned."

I'd spent the whole afternoon trying to figure out what Murphy had been thinking. Was her plan to make Olivia fall in love with the *Book of Houses* so she'd keep inviting Murphy over to her wonderful house, now that their math project was done? Or did she think one look at the *Book of Houses* would transform Olivia into a poem of air and light, an old soul, a good queen in a fairy tale?

"I know you're sorry, but who cares?" I said, idly picking up a pair of scissors and putting them down again. "I know I don't."

Murphy unzipped her backpack and pulled out the *Book of Houses*. Even in the late afternoon's half-light anyone could see it was in tatters. She lay the book in her lap and looked at it a minute without saying anything.

"I've thought about it all afternoon. We have to get rid of the books, Maddie." Murphy leaned forward and looked at me, solemn as Sunday morning. "I'm afraid their magic is gone after everything that happened this afternoon."

"The books aren't magic," I said dully. "They're just books."

Murphy stood up, cradling the *Book of Houses* tightly to her chest. "How can you say there's no magic in this book? Without it, the fort never would have been built. Without this book, Logan would still be halfway between this world and that one. The books brought him all the way over here to us. He's not the same person, and that, believe it or not, is magic."

She began to pace. "You saw Olivia today, when she first looked at the *Book of Houses*. For a minute she was a different person. She was . . ." Murphy fumbled for the right word.

"Human?"

"She was the real Olivia," Murphy replied. "The good Olivia, the one who watches stars. That was magic, too."

Then the air seemed to go right out of her. She fell back into the armchair. "My parents researched this group of Tibetan monks once. If one of their sacred objects even touched the ground, they got rid of it. That's how they honored their special things. They believed it was better to destroy something than to keep it when it was less than perfect."

I walked over to the box where my curtains lay in a jumble and pulled them out. I was too mad, just flat out too hurt, to think straight. Maybe if my head had been clearer, I would have seen certain things. I would have realized Murphy had lost something, too. Her dream of Olivia's house was gone. There'd be no more visits, no more light and air and poetry, no more stars seen through a glass ceiling.

But then, even if I'd realized it, I would have thought her loss nothing compared to mine. Because in my eyes, even if she never saw that house again, Murphy still had everything. She had the memory of parents who had loved her and taken her with them when they left for someplace new. She had tales of exotic lands and polished, blue stones hanging over her bed. She was special, a shining star for all to see.

Me, all I had were those books, and they were no good to me now. How could I ever pick up one of them again without hearing those voices laughing and yelling across the cafeteria? How could my books ever be special to me again?

"I don't care what you do with the books," I told her. "Do whatever you want."

And then Murphy was opening the box with the *Book of People* and all of our supplies in it, and then she was walking outside. "Come on," she called, but I just stood there. She came back and grabbed my hand, and I followed her like a girl in a dream.

The fact was, no matter how mad I was at Murphy, I'd go wherever she told me to.

She handed me both of the books, said, "Wait here for two minutes," and ran in the direction of Logan's house. I thought maybe she was going to get him and tell him to come take the books and hide them in his house, so that we wouldn't have to look at them anymore.

But when Murphy returned she was carrying a shovel she must have gotten from the Parrish's toolshed. She motioned me to follow her, and we tracked through the woods until we reached the fence separating the subdivision from Hampton's Dairy Farm, right at the edge of the trees. "I used to help my mom garden," Murphy said, beginning to dig. "Mostly I weeded, but first thing in the spring I helped her turn over the soil."

Within no time she dug a good-sized hole. It took me a second to realize that what I was feeling was scared, like we were about to bury a person, someone we'd murdered.

"Put the books in the hole," Murphy told me, and that's when I started to cry. I didn't know why I was crying. The books were no good to me anymore. Why save them? But I couldn't make myself hand them over to Murphy, even if the books were ruined.

"Come on, Maddie," she said gently, laying her hand on my shoulder, and I let my fingers loosen a little bit. I was tired and jumbled up with anger and sadness, and suddenly I just wanted to be done with the whole mess, the laughing voices and the torn pages and Olivia Woods' closed-down face. Sometimes things get too twisted up for you to hold on to them anymore; I guess that's the reason I handed those books over to Murphy. She took them from me and buried them deep in the hole and shoveled the dirt back over them.

"This is for the best," she said, and then turned and ran a few feet before throwing the shovel into the woods. "I'll come back tomorrow and put the shovel in the shed," she promised. Then she held out her hand, palm up, to the sky.

"It's starting to rain," she said. "We'd better run for it."

Chapter 20

That night everyone in the dorm went over to the dining hall to watch a movie they were showing on a big screen, a cartoon about the headless horseman. I didn't have the heart for it. I had no idea what Murphy and I would tell everyone when they discovered that the books were gone: dead and buried.

I doodled in my notebook, trying to come up with a good lie. What if Murphy and I acted surprised, like we thought the books had been stolen? My heart lifted with this idea, then fell. Why would anyone steal the books? Logan and Donita were too smart to fall for that sort of story.

I couldn't even bear to think about Ricky Ray.

Murphy stayed in the room, too, claiming that

she needed to study for a math test, but she was lying across her bed staring up at that blue stone as if she were hoping to fly away on the next strong wind.

"I think we should go dig up the books," I told her. I was starting to get a panicky feeling inside of me. I couldn't think of one good lie to tell Logan, Donita, and Ricky Ray. Besides, even if I didn't care about the books anymore, they still did. They were going to kill me when they found out what happened.

Murphy didn't even bother looking at me. "They're probably already ruined with all of this rain."

"Maybe not," I said. "Maybe there's still time to get them."

Finally Murphy turned to face me. "Let it go, Maddie. The books are gone. It's for the best."

Electric tingles ran up my arms and legs, and my face felt hot. I thought back to the first day I'd shown Murphy the books. I should have run the minute she and Logan had walked in the room. I should've shoved them under my bed and never let anyone, not even Ricky Ray, look at them.

No one's stopping me from going back to the fort, I told myself, but I stayed put, feeling frozen again, unable to make anything happen. I picked up my sketchbook and made criss-cross lines over an entire page, humming tunelessly.

I'd been doodling for almost half an hour, when a woman tapped on the half-open door to our room. She was pale and thin, dressed in a navy blue skirt and scuffed blue shoes. She'd covered her dark curls with a scarf. You could tell that once upon a time she'd been pretty, but her lipstick and eye shadow couldn't hide all the tired lines around her eyes and mouth.

"Emily?" the woman said, her voice sounding shy and hopeful.

"I'm sorry," I told her, "there's no Emily who lives here."

But she didn't seem to hear me. "Emily?" she said again, looking straight at Murphy. "Baby? Gosh, I've missed you so much."

And Murphy turned and looked out the window.

"I don't know what you're talking about," she said.

*   *   *

And then it was raining and raining and raining, a cold, end-of-October rain that made the leaves slippery on the path through the woods, and I was wearing tennis shoes so I slipped and slid and fell. I thought I would never get there, and I was afraid I wouldn't be able to find what I was looking for when I did.

But the turned-over earth was still fresh on top of the hole Murphy dug, and even though it was dark, dark, dark, I could see enough to dig through it with my bare hands to get to the books. *Please let them be okay*, I thought, *please let them be okay*.

But they weren't okay. I couldn't even turn the pages, they were soaked through with rain and stuck together, and I could have tried forever to dry them out and still they would never be right.

I didn't know what to do except make my way through the trees to the fort, where there was a flashlight, so I could take a closer look at how bad the damage was.

"She's not really my mother," Murphy'd said to me as soon as the woman left. "She just says she is. They made me live with her."

"Who did?"

"My real parents. At least, I think that's what must have happened. I think when I was very young, they left me with her, and they meant to come back to get me."

Murphy looked away. "That's what I think must have happened."

I didn't know what to say. I had the facts right in front of me, but they couldn't get inside my brain.

That woman was Murphy's mother.

Murphy's mother was not dead.

Her parents were not researchers.

They had never taken her to Africa. Or South America. Or New Mexico.

"You would hate my house, Maddie," Murphy'd said after a few minutes. "It's made out of cinder blocks. The floor is covered with old linoleum that's peeling up around the edges. I scrubbed and scrubbed, but I could never get that floor clean."

I picked up the *Book of Houses* and pointed the flashlight at it, hoping this time the pages would float free from each other and there would be Ricky Ray's castle and Logan's brick ranch house, there would be Donita's white cottage with the picket fence and garden and Russell's mural on the walls, and on the last two pages I'd find Murphy's castle in its enchanted forest. But the book was a soggy mess.

I walked back to the spot just beyond the woods, and this time I placed the books in the hole as gentle as could be, and I said, Goodbye, goodbye, and I knew I was saying goodbye to more than just the books as I scooped up the wet earth and placed it over them.

"So did you really fly? That time you jumped off of your porch?" I'd asked Murphy, back in the room.

Murphy nodded. "That really happened," she said softly. "I really did fly."

I sat down on my bed across from her and stared at my shoes. She tapped my foot lightly with hers and said, "You believe me, don't you?"

"No," I said after a minute. "I guess I don't."

And then Murphy was gone.

Chapter 21

November showed up cold and wet. On the bus to school, kids sniffled and sneezed and laid their heads against the windows, peering out through the rain to the skeleton trees. Christmas seemed a long way away, and spring was just a lie someone told you once that you didn't really believe. I carried a book with me everywhere and avoided making eye contact. I wasn't in the mood to communicate with anyone.

There was a hole inside of me. At first I thought it was just because the books were gone. But then I figured it had probably been there my entire life, starting from the time my mama left me. Granny Lane and Mr. Willis had filled it, but when I had to leave Roan Mountain, there was that hole again, only now it was bigger because it was the size of three people gone, not just one. It got a little bigger each time I had to say goodbye to someone I cared for.

After Murphy left the Home, and Donita and Logan discovered what happened to the books and stopped talking to me, well, I was pretty sure that hole was so big that it had eaten me up entirely. Teachers commented that I seemed real quiet lately, and then they stopped noticing me at all.

Walking around Elizabethton in rainy November is nobody's idea of a good time, but that's what I did, just to get out of my room in the afternoons. It had been a long while since I'd spent any time roaming around by myself. Even before the fort and Murphy and Logan and Donita, there'd been Ricky Ray, who was always ready to hike up to the Mini-Mart or spin in crazy circles on the swings. Sometimes on my walks I thought I could hear him running up behind me, keeping count of my footsteps for me, saying, When my mama comes to get me, you can come live with us. You can have the top bunk.

Of course, when I turned around, there was nobody there. But I kept turning around anyway, just out of habit.

It was my own fault I was all alone, I kept telling myself as I trudged along, my hands jammed hard into my pockets. Why wouldn't Logan and Donita be mad at me? And I couldn't bring myself to go knock on Ricky Ray's door, even though he'd already knocked on mine a half-dozen times. The idea of somebody as sweet as Ricky Ray being nice to me after I'd been so stupid made me cringe further into my jacket, as if a cold wind had slapped me across the face.

I'd start my afternoon at the library, trading out old books for new ones, then I'd shuffle over to the Limestone Grocery to buy a bag of chips. If Mr. Trivette was in his tiny office, I'd stop and pass some time with him until a customer came by for some coal, and then I'd make my way up the hill to Potter's Used Auto Parts and Misc. Supplies and stand under the sloping roof until Mr. Potter saw me and knocked on the window for me to come inside.

"Now, Maddie, you don't have to wait for an invitation," he'd say, ushering me through the front door and putting two quarters in the Coke machine. "You're always welcome here." Then he'd hand me a soda and say, "You're one of the best workers I've got."

"Mr. Potter, you don't have any employees," I'd tell him. "So I don't know how high a compliment that is."

"If I was hiring, I'd hire you, little gal," he always said.

Most times, I'd go into the storeroom and putter around a bit, take some inventory for Mr. Potter or start on my homework. Sometimes I'd take my sketchbook out of my backpack and draw for awhile and think. I thought a lot about Murphy, trying to sort through my feelings. I spent a long time wondering which of the things she'd told me were true and which were lies. Oh, I knew what the obvious lies were, the lies about her parents and about her aunt in Europe. But what about that boy who whispered poetry to horses?

I really wanted that story to be true.

I'd learned a lot about Murphy in the past weeks, things Corinne told me, even though she worried she shouldn't out of respect for Murphy's privacy. I learned that Murphy's daddy died from cancer when she was eight, and after that her mama fell all to pieces, drinking and laying out from her secretarial job. Murphy was the one who took care of things then, who went to the Winn-Dixie to buy the groceries and came home and cooked them up for dinner. She kept the house clean and got the laundry done. She'd been voted "Smartest Girl" in her fifth grade class. She never missed a day of school. Sometimes her mama hit her, but mostly she just watched TV and drank. Murphy's mama'd been in jail three times for driving drunk. Murphy had been in other foster-care homes. Her last foster-family had been well-off, which accounted for all of Murphy's nice stuff.

"So why's Social Services letting Murphy's mama take her back?" I asked Corinne one afternoon when I'd cornered her in the dorm kitchen and made her talk about it some more. "It sounds like she's got too many problems to take care of a child."

"It's important that families be reunited whenever possible," she said, picking up a plate from the dish drainer and drying it with a soft towel. "And it's true that Murphy's mother has serious problems with substance abuse, but she completed a rehabilitation program and is willing to spend the next six months in a halfway house with Murphy. They'll talk to counselors, and Murphy's mom will work on her issues."

"And then she'll take Murphy home and sit around getting drunk some more," I complained. I grabbed a bowl out of the drainer and began rubbing it hard with the hem of my shirt. "Not that I care what happens to her."

Corinne gently took the bowl from me and set it down on the counter. "The judge thinks Murphy's mother will do a better job this time," she said. "And the social workers think she can learn how to take care of Murphy."

"What do you think?" I asked, slumping into a chair.

"Well, I've read Murphy's files," Corinne said. She held up a fork to examine it, rubbed it on her sleeve, and turned away from me.

I came over to the sink and stood close to her. "What? What do *you* think, Corinne?"

"I think it's a long road, Maddie," she said finally.

"For Murphy and her mom?"

"For everyone."

* * *

One afternoon after it had been raining for days and days, Mr. Potter came into the back room where I was doing my math homework and said, "How's that fort holding up in all this bad weather?"

I shrugged. "I don't know. I haven't been up there in awhile."

"You children lose interest? That comes as a surprise, seeing how much work y'all put in up there."

"Well, you know, the weather and everything," I said lamely. "It's a long walk in bad weather."

"Fort's the best place in weather like this," Mr. Potter insisted, "if the structure's holding firm and the roof's not leaking. Dress up in some warm clothes, and you can have a fine afternoon in a fort."

Some odd expression must have crossed my face, because Mr. Potter came over to where I was working and put his hand on my shoulder. "You don't go on account of Murphy being gone, is that it?"

"I guess that's partly it," I said.

I'd told Mr. Potter some of the story, not about the books, but about Murphy's mother coming to get her, and how they were in a halfway house now, learning how to be a family. I didn't tell him that

Donita wouldn't speak to me anymore. I was afraid he'd feel like he shouldn't let me come to the shop.

Mr. Potter picked up a box of oil filters and lifted the lid, taking a moment to count its contents. "All I know is the weather's supposed to clear up tomorrow or the next day," he said. "You ought to go check on that fort. It's a shame to let such a fine place go to waste. I believe Murphy would agree with me on that account."

I grabbed the clipboard with the inventory list on it and pretended to study it. "I'll give that some thought, Mr. Potter," I said, trying to sound like I was about to get real busy with work. "I sure will."

Mr. Potter made a growly uh-huh sound, but he let me be. I paced around the storeroom, checking things off the list, listening to the rain. Every once in awhile I'd pull out Murphy's blue stone from my pocket and roll it around between the palms of my hands. She'd given it to me right before she left, saying she guessed I knew it wasn't really a rare and valuable artifact. She said she'd gotten it at the gift shop of a nature museum and made a lot of wishes on it that hadn't come true yet, but they might still someday.

When I held it, that stone didn't seem nearly as mysterious as it had hanging from the ceiling in our room like some distant planet. Up close it was more gray than blue. If you looked at it hard enough, it was hardly a cut or two above ordinary. I thought it about it awhile and decided it was a whole lot like me. Nothing special.

I guess you could say the same thing about Murphy. She was just a regular old foster-care child, no better or worse than any of us. I rolled that idea around my brain like a polished, blue stone, but it wouldn't settle into a spot where I could get used to it. Maybe I was as mad as mad can be when it came to Murphy, and maybe I was hurting a little bit about her being gone, too. The fact was, it would be a long time before I'd sort out who in the world Murphy was.

That didn't mean I didn't miss her.

I slipped Murphy's stone back into my pocket, wishing she'd stayed long enough for me to think of something good to give to her. But five minutes after she'd set the blue stone on my desk, she was gone. *I should have given her my rodeo belt buckle,* I thought, leaning my head against the window.

Maybe there was some place I could mail it to where Murphy would be sure to get it.

I turned my head and looked out at the cold, gray sky. Wrong time of the year for the fort, I told myself. A picture of Logan, Donita and Ricky Ray sitting up there cutting up and telling stories flashed in my brain, but I pushed it out and pushed it out again. It kept coming back in, though, and that hole inside me got a little bit bigger every time it did.

Chapter 22

When Mrs. Lyman yelled at me during JM practice that if I didn't get my nose out of that book, she was going to make me props manager instead of an active team participant, I put my book away in my backpack. Even though I wasn't in the mood to run around on stage solving impromptu problems and pretending to fly in our silver time machine, I didn't want to jeopardize my JM career for the next two and a half years of middle school.

I didn't even bother looking over at Logan for his reaction. I already knew he was wearing a sour look beneath the shadow of his Fraley's Feeds cap. He'd been wearing that same expression ever since he learned that Murphy and I'd buried the books. "We could have fixed the *Book of Houses,*

Maddie," he'd said. "We could have put it back together again."

"That book was way beyond fixing," I told him, but he didn't understand. And a few days later, when he found out Murphy was gone, that she wasn't even Murphy, he couldn't understand that either.

"How could she do that to me?" he kept repeating. We were sitting on the steps of the Older Girls' Dorm, the sky going dark above our heads.

"Do what?" I asked. "It wasn't her idea to go. They made her go."

Logan scooped up a handful of dirt and threw it into the yard. "I wish she'd never come here in the first place."

After that's when he stopped talking to me.

I was up on stage doing an improvisation exercise with Kenny Ehrlich, when a woman walked into the auditorium and took a seat in one of the rows toward the back. Because she looked young and was fashionably dressed, the first thing that came to my mind when I saw her was *talent scout*. Some sponsors from the First Baptist Church of Elizabethton had taken a group from our dorm to a play the weekend before, and I was still under its spell. I guess that's why I got it in my head that that woman was in the Lawton Crockett Middle School auditorium looking for talented eleven-year-olds.

The idea that there might be a talent scout in the audience put a little bit of zing back into my step. I'd spent three weeks being eaten up by the hole inside of me, and all of a sudden I felt like fighting back.

Before that moment I'd never really thought about being an actor, but suddenly I was filled up with the idea. It took the cold, rainy month of November, wrung it out, dried it up, and lit a fire in the fireplace. I turned to face Kenny Ehrlich, who I was supposed to be doing an improvisation with, and said funny, smart things that made him break character and crack up.

I was a star! At least that's how I felt up there making everyone laugh, all the lights on me.

Mrs. Parrish laughed and smiled as I babbled on about my newfound love of theater on our way to the Home. She still gave me a ride after every JM practice, even though Logan could barely bring himself to speak to me. For the past three weeks, Mrs. Parrish and I had made small talk, careful not to say anything that would highlight the fact that Logan currently couldn't stand the sight of me.

"You'll be a wonderful actress, Maddie," Mrs. Parrish told me as she pulled into the Home's driveway. "You have that necessary joie de vivre. That's something no actress can fake."

Logan snorted. It wasn't a snort that made a whole lot of sense to me, since I couldn't imagine why he would have an opinion on my joie de vivre, whatever that was. Maybe Logan's was more of a general issue snort, a snort that meant to express his overall dissatisfaction with the fact I was alive.

"I wish you two would make up and be friends again," Mrs. Parrish said, making a right-hand turn on Allen Avenue. "It seems like such a waste, the two of you not talking to each other. You've worked so hard together. That fort you children built, why, it's a marvel."

She brushed a strand of hair behind her ear, her fingers fluttering like she was nervous about something. "You know, I went up there again the other day."

"To the fort? By yourself?" Logan asked, clearly astonished.

"Yes, to the fort. I . . . well, I was worried. Logan, you never seem to go up there anymore, and you won't say a word to Maddie. What was I supposed to think?"

I leaned forward. "Did you look inside?" It'd been awhile since I'd been inside the fort. I hoped everything was still okay.

Mrs. Parrish nodded. Her face in the rear-view mirror was suddenly glowing like someone had shone a light on it. "It's beautiful, what you all have done up there! I'd never really taken a good look around before. The word *fort* doesn't do it justice. Why, you've built your own house."

"Logan did most of the work building it," I said, wondering if a compliment would soften him up any.

"No I didn't. Everybody worked on it," he said in a stiff voice, not giving an inch.

I shrugged. "Well, you were the one who taught us how to do it, pretty much. You and Mr. Potter."

"His grandfather taught him, you know," Mrs. Parrish said to me. "I looked at that fort, and

I thought, *A part of my father lives on out here*. It gave me goose bumps, it honestly did."

Logan stared straight ahead, but I saw the back of his neck turn red. And then I saw Mrs. Parrish do something I'd never seen her do before. Still keeping her eyes on the road, she reached over and brushed her fingers through Logan's hair.

"I was so impressed, honey," she said. "I'm really very proud of you."

Logan leaned his head into his mother's hand, letting it rest there for a moment before he sat up straight again.

I wanted so bad to put my hand on his shoulder, like I could be a part of his family, all proud of him, but I was afraid he'd just shrug it away. I didn't blame him one bit. I'd be furious with me, too.

But I told myself that soon I would be so caught up in my new life in the theater that I wouldn't have time to worry about it anymore. After Mrs. Parrish dropped me off, I floated down the hallway to my dorm room, imagining myself on stage receiving bouquets of roses and standing ovations. Donita and Kandy were at their desks studying, and I ignored them and they ignored me and we all ignored each other—and it didn't matter because I was going to be a star.

Corinne stuck her head inside the room just as I was unloading my books from my backpack to my bed. "So Maddie, did you meet Penny today?"

"Who?" I asked. "Oh, do you mean the talent scout?"

Corinne looked puzzled. "Hmmm, I don't know about a talent scout. But Penny Korda was supposed to come by your practice today and introduce herself."

She looked around the room, then gestured at me to come out into the hallway. "I guess I should tell you what's going on," she half-whispered as she led me down the hall to the living-room. "Penny contacted the Home a few weeks ago because she's interested in adopting an older child. She's single, but she has a good job and could provide a lot for a child your age, with your interests."

I stopped. "She wants to adopt me?"

"She wants to get to know you," Corinne said. "To see if you two would make a good match."

I didn't seem to be a good match with anyone

these days, so why should things work out with this Penny Korda person? It was probably a lost cause. Thinking about it some more, it came to me that Ricky Ray was the one who needed a mama. I'd gotten along fine for eleven years without one, but Ricky Ray was still a little boy who needed taking care of.

"She should adopt Ricky Ray," I told Corinne. "I bet she'd like him a lot."

"She's looking to adopt an older girl, eleven, twelve, thirteen. Ricky Ray doesn't fit the bill, I'm afraid," Corinne said. "By the way, where's he been lately? For awhile I thought he lived here."

"He's off with the rest of the six-year-olds," I said lightly. "Being six."

Corinne put her hand on my shoulder. "You know, you're eligible for adoption, Maddie. This could be a great opportunity for you."

Back in my room I lay across my bed, my theater dreams taken over by the idea of being adopted. I wanted to talk about it with somebody, but Donita was out of the question. She shared Logan's bad feelings when it came to me. After she and Logan had gone to the fort and found the books gone, she'd come back to the dorm wanting to know what happened to them. I'd led her to where they were buried.

"Maybe those books were yours to begin with," she said after staring at the mound of dirt for a few moments. "But they became our books. Ours, as in a group of people who were friends. You had no right to do what you did."

"They were just books," I told her, "just pictures we cut out."

Donita glared at me. "That's a lie, and you know it's a lie better than anybody else in this world."

Then she kicked her toe into the dirt, digging out a little hole. "We should have known all along about that girl, I guess," she said, almost like she was talking to herself. "She told us right up front she wasn't who she said she was."

"What do you mean?"

"First day she was here, she said Murphy wasn't her real name. Should've known the rest of it was lies, too."

I rolled over on my bed and put my face in my pillow, which made me think that if I got adopted, I'd probably have nice new sheets on my bed that smelled like fabric softener. The pillowcase where my face now resided was a hand-me-down from someone at church and was probably twenty years old, and it smelled like industrial strength detergent, the kind you use when you're washing the sheets from seventy-five beds.

That pillowcase did me in. Two seconds after I rolled off the bed and hopped to my feet, I was knocking on Corinne's door.

"Tell that Penny person that the next time she stops by, she ought to say hello," I said the minute Corinne popped her head out. "Tell her she ought not be such a stranger."

Chapter 23

When I was just a baby, a ghost saved my life. This is according to my Granny Lane, who I lived with at the time in a trailer on Roan Mountain.

I told this story to Penny Korda about fifteen minutes after I first met her. We were sitting at the table for eleven-year-old girls, eating meat loaf that looked like it wore out its welcome in the oven by a good half hour.

When I finished telling my ghost story to Penny Korda, I could tell she found me worth getting to know better. I tried to keep her interested by being interested in her. "Tell me about your job," I said. "What do you do for a living?"

Penny Korda took a sip of her iced tea and said, "I teach art part-time in Knoxville. When I'm not teaching, I illustrate children's books."

"Could you teach me how to draw hands?" I asked her. "I can draw faces, but not hands."

"Hands are tough," Penny Korda agreed. She took my hand and pointed out the various features that make hands one of the harder things to get down on paper, and then she got a pencil out of her bag and started sketching on a napkin. She sketched with her left hand and ran her right hand through her short hair as she drew, making it stick up all over the place. She reminded me of Mr. Willis.

After dinner was over, Penny asked if I'd be interested in spending a weekend at her house in Knoxville. "You can play with my art supplies," she said, smiling. "I have a whole room full of them."

I tore a piece of my napkin and scrunched it into a little ball. I wanted like anything to go to Penny's house, but all of a sudden I got to thinking about Ricky Ray again. I couldn't just leave him behind, could I? I mean, who would he have left if I up and moved to Knoxville?

Penny leaned over the table toward me. "We don't

have to decide anything yet, okay? It's just for a weekend. If that works out, then we'll try another weekend, and then another weekend."

I considered this. "Some weekend, do you think I could bring a friend with me?"

Penny laughed. "Sure," she said. "Just give me advance warning so I can make sure I have enough clean towels."

"He won't care," I told her, my heart lifting up a million miles. I was pretty sure clean towels weren't high on Ricky Ray's list of important things.

At bedtime I tried to go to sleep, but I was too excited thinking about going to visit Penny Korda to even get a yawn out. I tried to imagine what her house might look like, an old Victorian maybe, with hidden rooms and secret passageways. Or maybe it was a new house with cathedral ceilings and a Jacuzzi in the master bath. My hand started itching, it was wanting to cut out pictures so bad.

Which was why, the next day, I went with Corinne to the Winn-Dixie and picked up three real estate guides from the free publications rack. While Corinne was standing in the checkout line, I raced over to the drugstore to buy a notebook and some scissors and glue and a copy of *Southern Living*, which always had great house pictures in it. Then, as soon as Corinne pulled into the parking space behind the Older Girls' Dorm, I was out of the van like a flash and running up Allen Avenue, over Dewey Payne Road, and a quarter mile through the woods that ran along the edge of Hampton's Dairy Farm. The leaves had all fallen down, so I could see the fort from far away. I ran so hard I could barely breathe, but breathing didn't matter. I just wanted to get there, to sit down on the floor, to cut out one picture after another until my book was filled up with them.

I ran and I ran, and the minute I got there I leaped up the steps to the fort and pushed my way through the door.

Logan, Donita, and Ricky Ray were already there.

They were sitting on the floor wrapped in their winter coats, laughing and talking, pens and pencils and notebooks all around. And there, on the west window, were my yellow curtains, uneven and pretty, catching a breeze that was blowing through the fort.

"What are you doing here?" Logan asked. His voice wasn't mean or angry, which surprised me. Mostly he just sounded curious.

I held up the plastic bag from the Winn-Dixie filled with my supplies, as though Logan would be able to tell from the weight of it what it contained. "I'm starting a new book," I told him. "This seemed like the right place to do it."

"We started new books, too!" Ricky Ray said, his voice sweet and eager. "Only they're kind of different than the ones we did before."

I moved closer to their circle, curious. "Oh, yeah? How so?"

Logan picked up one of the books so I could see it up close. It was a notebook filled with graph paper, and on the page he showed me, I saw that he'd drawn an elaborate floor plan.

"I thought it would be fun if we tried designing some houses," Logan said. "We wouldn't build them or anything. It's just fun coming up with the plans."

Ricky Ray patted the floor beside him, and I took a seat. "I'm just kind of drawing stuff," he said. "I can't do plans the way Logan does." He showed me each of the pictures he'd drawn: a castle, a mansion, a ranch with a strange-looking horse tied up outside.

"Those are really good, Ricky Ray," I told him. I snuggled up to him a little, and suddenly he was sitting in my lap. "I'm real sorry about everything," I whispered to him, and he nodded.

"I know it," he said. "It's okay."

Penny Korda was going to like Ricky Ray, I just knew it. And if she didn't, well, that was too bad. Because I wasn't going anywhere without him; I was pretty sure about that.

You're taking a big risk, a voice inside of me said. *You might be stuck here forever.*

I looked around the fort. It wasn't the house of my dreams, but as long as my friends were here, it would do. Maybe we could still paint that mural we'd been talking about. Maybe one day we could invite some folks over for a party.

I smiled, thinking about who we might invite. Mr. Potter, for sure, and could be we'd extend an invitation to old Mr. Trivette and to Mrs. Dugger over at the library. And Penny Korda was welcome to come visit, too. I had a feeling she might like it out here in the middle of the woods.

Thinking about a party and all the friends we'd invite, well, I felt that hole inside of me get a little bit smaller. I leaned over toward Donita, my expression daring her to ignore me. "So are you doing house plans, too?"

She shook her head. "I'm more interested in what's inside the houses," she said. She flipped through the pages of her notebook until she found a picture she liked enough to show me. It looked like a design for a theater set, showing where every chair should be put and where the table was and so on.

"Wow," I said. "That's great."

Donita shrugged. "I'm not that good at drawing. But it's fun to come up with the plans. I like to think about how different people would set up their houses in different ways."

"What do you have in the bag, Maddie?" Ricky Ray asked, poking his pencil at it.

I dumped out the real estate guides and the scissors and glue and the notebook. "I was going to start another *Book of Houses*," I told him. "But now I don't know."

"You should do our idea," he said.

"It's a good idea," I agreed with him. I walked over to the trash can to throw away my bag. Seeing those glittery, gold swirls and twirls made my throat feel tight. "I bet Murphy would have liked it, too," I said, squeezing my hands together hard, hoping that a little hurt might keep out a bigger one.

"You think she'll ever come back, Maddie?" Ricky Ray asked. "You think we'll ever see her again?"

"Who cares?" Logan said. "She was a liar and a fraud."

"Maybe," I said. "But she knew how to tell good stories."

That cracked Donita up. She laughed so hard she was wiping tears out of her eyes. "I guess you got a point, Maddie," she said finally. "Liar, storyteller, it's all the same thing, ain't it?"

"It kind of is," I insisted, not sure what I was trying to say. "Maybe she had to tell those lies to make herself feel better. And after awhile she believed them so much they were the truth to her."

"But they were still lies," Logan said, not budging. "She wanted us to believe things about her that weren't true."

"No," said Donita, serious now, figuring things out. "*She* wanted to believe things that weren't true. Maybe it wasn't all that important whether we believed 'em or not."

I nodded my head. That was it. That's why I couldn't hate Murphy. All those stories she told, each one was a little dream she had about herself, about who she might've been, if her luck had been better, if those parents she wanted to believe in so badly had ever come back to get her.

"I heard you're getting adopted," Donita said, turning back to her notebook. "By that lady who ate dinner with us last night. Is that true?"

"I don't know. Maybe."

"Can I come stay with you sometimes?" Ricky Ray asked.

"Just wait and see," I told him, leaning into him.

I picked up my notebook and reached over Donita to grab a pencil. I smiled at her as I sat back down, and she smiled at me. "My mama's coming to see me next weekend," she told me. "Maybe I'll get to go home before too long."

"Is Rita coming, too?" I asked.

Donita rolled her eyes. "That girl is such a mess.

She better come. But she's got this boy now; he's all she can talk about."

Logan laughed. "You're just jealous she's got a boyfriend and you don't," he said. Donita leaned over and socked him on the arm, and I opened my notebook to the first page. I was going to try to draw a picture of Penny Korda's face from memory. I'd give it to her when she came to pick me up to take me to her house in Knoxville, and she'd be so impressed she wouldn't mind that Ricky Ray was coming along for the ride.

I drew one picture and then I drew another. First I drew Penny's face, and then, for the first time since I don't know when, I made a sketch of Granny Lane, her hand on her hip, her mouth opening to give Mr. Willis some sass. A parade of people started coming out of my pencil: Randy Nidiffer, Mr. Willis, Logan and Donita, the two of them cutting up about something as usual.

I drew as fast as I could, trying to keep up with my imagination. A house burst onto the paper. That's where everyone was walking to, and there was me and Ricky Ray on the front porch, waving as they strolled up the driveway.

In my mind I could see my mama walking up the street, her light brown hair floating around her face, and there was a man behind her who I just knew was my daddy, his blue eyes just like mine.

It was a family reunion; I saw it clear as day. Which was why it was no surprise when Murphy flew onto my paper, her head thrown back, her arms stretched out against the sky.

About the Author

Frances O'Roark Dowell is the editor of *Dream/Girl*, a critically acclaimed American arts magazine for girls. She received her MA in Poetry from the University of Massachusetts, and has published poems in several respected literary journals. Her other book for Walker, *Dovey Coe*, was a huge success and won several literary prizes in America, amongst them the US Edgar Award for Best Juvenile Mystery. It was hailed by the *Guardian* as "A delicately written account of life as an outsider in a rural American community in the twenties. Dovey is such a wonderful, strong character that she seems to speak directly to the reader, while the writing has the wistful quality of precious, long-distant memories."

Frances O'Roark Dowell lives in North Carolina with her husband and son.